# SECRETS BEYOND THE NILE

by A. R. Marshall

www.armarshall.com/storykeeping

## STORY KEEPING SERIES

BOOK THREE

To Aricin, Talia, and Oliver,

Go after your dreams like Charlotte.

**\*Note to Parents – FREE Audiobook!**

Thanks! You're going to love the Story Keeping Series!

As a token of my thanks I'm offering the AUDIOBOOK, *The Night I Became A Hero*, for FREE to my readers. I'll also keep you up to date on upcoming releases, special deals, and other freebies...

\*earbuds not included

Download for free at
*www.armarshall.com /storykeeping*

# Table of Contents

# Preface

Hi. My name is Riles.

In case you missed my first two stories - or maybe you read them a long time ago - here's a little bit about me so you feel caught up.

I am a hero. My sister and brother, too.

We can't fly. We don't have super speed, x-ray vision, plastic arms, or super strength. In fact, we're pretty normal in every way except one – we are *Story Keepers*.

Have you ever heard of *Story Keeping*? That's okay, neither had we - until that first summer at grandpa's house.

Every summer since I can remember, Sissie, Finn and I spend a week at grandpa's house. Mom and dad drop us off at the beginning of the week and pick us up seven days later. Over the years, we've had amazing adventures with grandpa – treasure hunts, night hikes, star-gazing, and s'mores around the backyard fire pit.

This summer grandpa took the adventures to a whole new level.

He introduced us to story keeping. You know how most stories have happy endings? I love rooting for happy endings.

Did you know that happy endings need help? Happy endings aren't guaranteed.

There are people out there, right now, trying to ruin stories by taking away the happy ending. Crazy, right?

Not everybody is trying to ruin stories though - grandpa says people have also been trying to save stories for centuries. Grandpa said his mom trained him to be a *Story Keeper*. She learned *Story Keeping* from one of her great uncles, or something. Now grandpa is teaching us!

When stories need saving, *Story Keepers* step in to help. I know, it sounds kind of silly, but it's true. We protect stories and save happy endings.

A few days ago, we had our first adventure, saving Drift Elwick from a mess of trouble on a spaceship parked between Earth and Mars. Last night I almost got stuck in the Middle Ages with a nasty magician and a whiny prince, but Sissie found a way to help me get home.

And today? Well, keep reading - you'll see. These adventures keep getting crazier. That's why Storytime is still my favorite part of the day.

Enjoy the adventure,

*-Riles*

# 1

## Breakfast

"Are they moving?" little Finn asked in a whisper, wide-eyed and staring.

Exhausted from adventures the night before, the three of us slept in *way* longer than usual. The smell of sizzling bacon woke us. It travelled a long way from the kitchen, and we each woke up with growling stomachs.

Now awake, we could hear grandpa scrambling eggs and flipping pancakes while humming a tune in the kitchen. All three of us jumped out of bed, threw on clothes, and headed to the kitchen at the same time.

Sliding across the bench, we all noticed it. Right there on the dining table - another book. The leather cover looked old and well-used, just like Drift's story, and Winthrop's. This book wore a sandy brown binding with a thick border of hieroglyphs decorating the front cover.

"Egyptian?" Sissie whispered.

Could be, I thought.

"Guys, seriously, I think they're moving!" Finn whispered a little louder.

He was right.

The hieroglyphs *were* moving - a twitch in a bird's wing, a blinking eye, a wriggle in a snake's body - all around the border.

In the middle of the cover, the hieroglyphic border framed a desert scene - small pyramids near the top, a winding blue line that stretched top to bottom, and a small red "X" near the lower left corner.

"A map?" The words slipped out of my mouth in a hushed whisper.

I turned to grandpa, "Do we get to read this one tonight?"

"Not exactly," grandpa called back over the whistle of his tea kettle.

Sissie looked up with her best pouty face, "So, you're teasing us?"

"Not exactly," grandpa chuckled.

He turned off the stovetop, loaded food onto four plates, and joined us at the table.

"Well, why *exactly* did you bring this book out?" little Finn asked.

"Hold that thought," grandpa smiled.

He headed back into the kitchen, returning a moment later with his favorite tea cup and three small glasses of juice.

"How about some breakfast?"

Really? How could we eat with this incredible book staring at us from the middle of the table?

"Grandpa?" we all whined.

"Alright, alright," he laughed. "I took the book out so we could read it... right after breakfast."

Exchanging glances, the three of us smiled wide, and began shoveling food into our mouths. Grandpa took his time, slowly sipping his steaming tea.

Between heaping shovels of syrup drenched pancakes, Little Finn must have chugged his juice a little too fast.

Suddenly, he let out a giant burp. It smelled like bacon. The burp made Sissie laugh so hard, that scrambled eggs started coming out her nose. Eggs should never come out of your nose.

After that, we all had the giggles - even grandpa.

After a hearty laugh, grandpa said, "No need to rush, the story will still be waiting for us when you finish."

We settled in and took our time. When we had all cleared our plates, we rinsed the dishes and grandpa poured himself another cup of tea. Finally, ready for another story, we all sat down around the table.

Little Finn shifted back and forth in his seat, as grandpa sipped his tea, "Do we really get to read this book today?"

"Yes, of course," grandpa smiled. Leaning in, he added, "but first, we need to talk."

"About last night?" I asked, barely looking up.

"Yes."

The three of us nodded. Things had not gone as planned. I glanced down at the caterpillar scar still fresh on my forearm, remembering.

"So," grandpa asked, "What did we learn from last night's adventure?"

"That story keeping is awesome?" little Finn smiled wide.

"Maybe," grandpa replied, "but what happened last night was *not* awesome. And, you fell asleep before the story ended, little one."

Finn blushed and smiled.

"What else?" Grandpa continued.

Sissie jumped in, "Grandpa, last night you kept a lot of secrets from us. That story was more dangerous than any of us thought."

"That's true, Sissie," grandpa replied.

"And more real," I added, looking again toward the scar on my arm.

"Also, true." Grandpa continued, "Now, what have we learned about *story keeping*?"

"Hmmm," little Finn thought for a moment, "We can help characters in the book."

"Yes. What else?"

"We can jump inside the story." I added, "And usually, we can move around inside the story."

"Good. What else?"

"We aren't the only ones jumping around in stories," Sissie added.

"Good Sissie," grandpa replied. "Go on."

Sissie sat tall, with a big smile. She really loved getting answers right.

"Well," she said, "the Lady of the Western Wood surprised me when she took our hands, flashed green, and moved us from the castle to her home in the cave!"

"It surprised me too," I added. "I didn't think she was one of us."

Little Finn interrupted, "Wait, the Lady of the Western Wood did that? When? I don't remember."

"That's because you fell asleep," grandpa chuckled.

"Oh yeah, right," Finn blushed again.

"Any other examples?"

"Well," I went on, "in the first book we met Lark, and in the second, we met Devlin. They both flash dark red."

"Good," grandpa replied.

"So, we've got green, and dark red," Sissie tallied the colors.

"Don't forget white," little Finn added, "you and Riles flash white."

"And grandpa too, right?" I added.

"Indeed," grandpa smiled. "Back to Lark and Devlin, what did we learn about them?"

"Lark wants to ruin happy endings," Sissie jumped in. "That's what she said in Drift's story."

"She also said she works for some Master," little Finn added.

"Master Calamitous?" I jumped in.

"Yes," grandpa confirmed.

"Wait a second," little Finn asked, "isn't that who Devlin said *he* worked for?"

"It is," grandpa answered.

"Really?" I asked. "I don't remember that."

"Me either," Sissie added.

Grandpa smiled, "That's because only Finn and I were outside the book when we learned it."

"Really?" I asked.

Finn nodded with a huge smile.

"So," I added, "I guess it helps to be outside the story sometimes?"

"Exactly," grandpa smiled.

Then, he put on one of those get-ready-to-learn-an-important-life-lesson looks that parents sometimes use and said, "Kids, I know it's exciting to jump inside these stories, but we can learn a lot both inside *and* outside the story."

"Okay," I smiled at grandpa. "What else do we need to know before we read this story?"

"Well," grandpa continued, "last night you learned to work together as a team, both inside and outside the book."

"Yeah, thanks guys," I said, looking at Sissie and Finn, "Without you two I'd still be inside that story."

"And," grandpa went on, "I won't be keeping as many secrets this time."

"Good," Sissie said in her mom voice.

"And," grandpa finished, "We're reading during the day, just in case the story takes longer than expected."

"Awesome-sauce," little Finn smiled, "Maybe this time I'll be able to stay awake!"

We all laughed.

Then, grandpa asked, "Shall we get started?"

## 2

## Dr. Bell

"So, grandpa," Finn asked, "Have you ever read this book before?"

"I have."

Grandpa lifted the book between his hands and placed the book on its spine. As he moved his hands apart, he let the sandy leather cover fall open. Dusty pages lit up with a soft white glow. They appeared to turn themselves, opening to a page near the front. When the pages stopped turning, grandpa adjusted his glasses and leaned over the book.

Sissie, Finn, and I watched amazed. Sure, we saw it happen with the other books, but do you ever get used to seeing a book turn its own pages? Let me tell you from personal experience - you don't.

"Here's a good spot," grandpa mumbled to himself, then looking across the table at us, "Are we ready?"

We all nodded, and grandpa started reading.

***

Dr. Charlotte Bell stood beside the starboard rail, atop the RMS Homeric - a tired trans-Atlantic cruise ship, spending its final days touring the Mediterranean. In her left hand, Charlotte held a medium sized leather suitcase. In her right, she clutched a small handbag.

She was the only passenger disembarking in Alexandria.

"So, this is Africa," Dr. Bell whispered to herself. They had sailed through the night to get here.

Far below her, the crew of the RMS Homeric secured the boat to a dock. Beyond the dock, the African port town of Alexandria bustled with merchants, automobiles, horse carts, and saddled camels.

Charlotte slowly drew in a deep breath. The salty sea breeze stirred her memory as it mixed with unfamiliar spices and fresh fish. She thought back to traveling with her father as a child. Was she ready for this adventure? She wondered.

Dr. Bell smiled nervously and scanned the horizon. In a few moments, she would take her first steps in Africa. She had dreamed of this moment for many years.

Beyond Alexandria, a sweeping desert stretched east - the mighty Sahara. Miles and miles of sand glistened like gold in the morning sunlight.

She set down her suitcase for a moment, and tugged a British passport from her shirt pocket. Thumbing it open, she read it to herself for the thousandth time: "Miss Charlotte Cook, of Liverpool."

"It'll be fine," she reassured herself in a whisper. "I can do this."

\*\*\*

"I thought her name was Dr. Charlotte Bell?" Sissie interrupted.

"Me too," I added.

"It is," grandpa replied.

Sissie and I exchanged confused looks.

"But the passport says Miss Charlotte Cook," I said.

"Yes, it does," grandpa nodded.

Sissie and I glanced at each other again, still confused.

"Egypt's where the pyramids are, right grandpa?" little Finn jumped in.

Grandpa smiled, "Yep. Shall I continue?"

We nodded.

*** 

"Miss Cook?"

Charlotte recognized the voice. She turned to face Chief Officer, First Mate Higgins.

"Everything is arranged," he smiled. "Are you ready?"

"Yes, of course," she replied. "Thank you, Stuart."

Chief Officer, First Mate, Stuart Higgins took hold of Dr. Bell's suitcase and led her through the ship's winding interior hallways. They worked their way down to level 3. There, they would access the gangway - a moving staircase leading from the ship to land.

Eventually, they stepped out of the dim hallway, into a wide room full of morning sunlight. Stuart led Charlotte to an important looking, short man standing behind a tall counter next to the gangway.

"Passport and papers, please," the short man said with no hint of smile.

"Yes, of course."

Dr. Charlotte Bell pulled the passport and papers from her handbag and slid them to the man in a suit. Her eyes drifted to the open doorway beyond his counter - to the gangway, to the dock, to Africa.

The man sifted the papers, glancing up at Dr. Bell a few times.

"Excellent, Miss Cook," the man said, glancing between Charlotte and the passport. "How long will you be staying in Alexandria?"

"No more than a few weeks, I suppose," Dr. Bell forced a smile.

"And, Miss Cook, are you aware of the current diplomatic challenges we are facing with Egypt?"

"I am."

She took another deep and nervous breath.

"Very well, Miss Cook" the man replied.

He signed the papers, firmly stamped her passport, and handed both back.

"Many thanks," Charlotte nodded.

She quickly returned the papers to her shirt pocket, retrieved her luggage from Stuart, and headed down the gangway stairs.

"One last thing, Miss Cook," the man offered.

Charlotte paused on the steps and looked back.

"Be careful," he said, smiling slightly, "and return home soon."

"Indeed," Charlotte winked at the man and headed down the long, narrow gangway.

Stepping onto the dock, she drew in another deep breath and let it out slowly. Then, she took her first steps in Africa.

***

"Grandpa, why did she wink?" Finn interrupted.

"And, what's her real name?" Sissie added.

Grandpa smiled, "Do you want me to tell you everything about the book before we even get there?"

"No, I guess not," Sissie said.

"Can we get back to the story?" grandpa asked.

We all nodded.

***

Even at sunrise, the heat and bustle of North Africa overwhelmed Charlotte. Merchants lined the dock with small shops - mostly tents - filled with fresh foods, spices, carved alabaster, and woven cloths. A mix of horse-drawn carriages and automobiles filled the roads, shuttling shoppers and businessmen this way and that.

Where the road began, row of taxis waited eagerly near the RMS Homeric, hoping to escort passengers from the cruise ship into the city center. Charlotte smiled. They were going to be sorely disappointed. She was the only passenger disembarking that morning.

# 3

## Alexandria

Setting her luggage down, Charlotte tugged a small train ticket from her handbag:

*Alexandria Station. Train 8. Departs 07:20 am. 1ˢᵗ Class, Express to Cairo. Car 4, Rm 6/7.*

Sliding the ticket back into her handbag, she waived at the first taxi in line. It rolled forward and an Egyptian man stepped out. His white pants and long white top contrasted sharply with his tanned skin. On his head he wore a small red cap.

"Where to, Madam?" He spoke with a clean English accent.

"Alexandria Station, please."

"Yes, Madam, of course."

The driver loaded Dr. Bell's luggage, helped her into the car, and began driving toward the train station. Charlotte stared out the window, entranced by the busy shops and overflowing cafés along the city streets. Alexandria was alive all around her - no longer a city in her imagination. She could hardly contain the excitement bubbling inside.

The driver noticed something. Something on the road behind them.

"You are traveling alone?"

"Yes."

Charlotte shifted in her seat, to watch the driver. He had a kind voice. His eyes glanced frequently in the side mirrors.

"It is a difficult time to be Africa," he offered, sounding concerned.

"Yes."

"You will be safe?"

"I hope so," she replied.

The driver pulled to the side of the road in front of the train station. Charlotte paid for the ride, adding a tip. Several young Egyptian boys raced to help her with the luggage. Each boy carried one end of her medium sized suitcase while she walked in front holding her handbag.

Behind her, on the street, the driver watched as a second car pulled up to the train station. Several men stepped out, their eyes on the woman - Miss Charlotte Cook.

*** 

"What's going on?" Sissie interrupted.

"She's getting on a train," I snapped. "Stop interrupting!"

"I know *that*, Riles," Sissie snapped back, "I mean what's going on with the driver and those other guys."

"Oh, right," I muttered.

"Are you two finished?" grandpa asked.

Finn laughed at Sissie and I for getting in trouble, and grandpa kept reading.

\*\*\*

Charlotte made her way to Train 8, moving quickly across the empty station. The boys followed fighting over who was carrying more of her suitcase. As she approached the train, an attendant took the suitcase from the boys and shooed them away. Dr. Bell gave both boys several coins for their work, and showed her ticket to the attendant.

"Room 6/7 on Car 4, please?" Charlotte spoke with confidence.

"Of course, Miss Cook," the attendant replied.

Carrying her suitcase, the attendant led Charlotte to Train Car 4. They stepped onto the train and walked along a narrow passage to Room 6/7. The attendant stepped into the room and placed her suitcase in the overhead bin. Then, he stepped into the hallway so Charlotte could enter.

Her private room had two couches facing each other, and a spacious window.

"Thank you, this is wonderful," Charlotte said, turning to the attendant.

"I'm glad you like it, Miss Cook."

She gave the attendant a generous tip, and a warm smile.

"Thank you, Miss Cook," he replied, "Safe travels."

"Indeed," she replied.

The attendant closed the door. Dr. Charlotte Bell waited quietly as his footsteps faded. Then, she locked the door, sat down on one of the couches and glanced out the window. The platform was nearly empty. Many of the travelers were Egyptian. A few were American. Others appeared to be French, German, and Greek. She also noticed several odd-looking British gentlemen a good distance away.

Were they talking to the boys who had carried her suitcase?

She drew the window curtains closed, just in case. Then, reaching into her handbag, she pulled out a small leather notebook.

Running her fingers across the leather binding, Charlotte's mind drifted. All those hours searching through old libraries and dusty old books. So much time collecting notes, translating hieroglyphs, and studying artifacts brought to England after the Great War.

All those clues lined the pages of this leather notebook: sketches, diagrams, symbols, names, dates, and quotes. So many puzzle-pieces leading her here - to Egypt, to the Nile, to the Valley of the Kings.

She could hardly believe her adventure was underway.

Just then, footsteps and whispers in the hallway interrupted her thoughts.

She stiffened.

A knock on the door. She ignored it.

"Miss Cook?" It was the attendant's voice, "The train will be leaving shortly."

"Many thanks," she replied, without getting up.

She tried to relax in her seat. Maybe there was nothing to worry about. *Perhaps a cup of tea would calm my nerves*, she thought.

Charlotte carefully placed the leather notebook back in her handbag.

*Yes,* she thought, *nothing to worry about. Some food and tea will do me good.*

She gathered herself, and headed into the hallway. The train whistled. Charlotte locked the door and turned just as her train car jerked forward. Losing her balance, Charlotte dropped her handbag, and her leather notebook slipped out.

Quickly, she tucked the notebook back into the handbag and stood up.

*Good*, she thought, *no one saw.*

At the far end of the car, she heard the train car door slide open and shut. Charlotte glanced that direction and saw two men step into her hallway. Were they the same two men she saw talking with her luggage boys? Charlotte couldn't tell.

She turned quickly and headed to the restaurant.

# 4

## Train Chase

"Grandpa, are those men following Charlotte?" Little Finn asked.

I wondered the same thing, but after snapping at Sissie for interrupting, I didn't want to ask any questions.

"I think we have to wait a bit to find that out," grandpa said with a smile.

"Is she in trouble?" Sissie asked.

"Well, it looks like she's the hero of the story, so she'll probably face *some* challenges along the way," grandpa answered.

"That makes sense," I chimed in.

"Now," grandpa went on, "how about we get back to reading the story?"

"Sounds good," we all answered.

***

Charlotte walked steadily through several train cars on her way to the restaurant. She passed a few empty rooms, and overheard many passengers settling into their accommodations.

One man passed her in the hallway. She kept her eyes low. He was tall and thin, and the smell of dark coffee clung to his coat.

***

"Grandpa?" I asked, after an unusually long pause in the reading.

He looked at all three of us, "What?"

"Are you going to keep reading?" Sissie asked. "You seemed to stop there."

"Sorry, I was just thinking," he paused again. "I'm not sure I remember reading about this man who smells like coffee before."

"The tall thin one?" Finn asked.

"Yes."

"What does that mean?" I asked.

"Should we be nervous?" Sissie wondered aloud.

"No, I probably just forgot about him," grandpa smiled. "So many stories, so many characters. Shall I continue?"

We nodded.

*\*\*\**

Finally, Charlotte arrived at the restaurant car. A rush of smells and sounds poured over her. Passengers filled nearly every table: eating, drinking, talking, and reading. Near the back of the car, she spotted a small, empty table with two chairs.

She made her way to that empty table, and sat facing the entrance.

The morning light brightened the car. The train had quickly escaped the edge of Alexandria, and the lush landscape beyond the city surprised her. Rather than the desert sand she expected, fertile farmland filled her view to the west and south.

The restaurant car had as much life as the farmland outside - passengers buzzing with excitement. Charlotte scanned the tables.

To Dr. Bell's left, a table of women in fancy dresses chatted about the theaters in Cairo. Behind them, a young Ethiopian family sat together. The father sipped tea in his traditional white tunic. The mother wore a brightly colored wrap. Their two young boys ate toast with perfect manners. To her right, a casually dressed American sipped his coffee and read his paper alone. Behind him, sat several European businessmen in stiff suits, discussing oil contracts. Were they French and German?

An Egyptian waiter made his way to her table, interrupting her observations.

"Good morning, Miss Cook."

"Good morning," Dr. Bell replied.

He handed her a menu and waited.

"Toast with jam, and coffee, please."

"Excellent," the waiter left with the menu.

At the entrance, a thick British man squeezed into the restaurant car. She recognized him right away. He *was* one of the men talking with her suitcase helpers.

He saw her too, and made a small wave in her direction.

She looked away immediately, pretending not to notice.

When she looked that direction again, she saw him walking directly toward her, apologizing to passengers as he bumped them along the way.

She held tightly to her handbag, and tried to relax. She expected something like this to happen.

"Hello, Miss Cook. May I?" he spoke with a rough English accent and pointed to the chair across from her.

Charlotte stiffened. *How does he know that name?* she thought.

The man removed his coat, hanging it over the chair, placed his bowler hat on the table, and sat. He had dark hair, a scruffy face, and light blue eyes. He wore a white button up, suspenders, and no tie.

The waiter returned with Charlotte's coffee and toast.

"Could I trouble you for some breakfast tea?" the man asked the waiter.

"Of course, sir."

When the waiter left, the man leaned forward. He pulled a small white card from his shirt pocket, placed it on the table, and slid it toward Charlotte.

"Take a peek, Miss Cook."

Then, he leaned back in his chair.

*Be brave*, she thought.

She slid the paper to the edge of the table and flipped it over in her lap so she could read it properly:

*Telegram, Urgent [21 Oct 1923]*

*Her Majesty's Intelligence Service: The doctor has assumed a new name. Needs safe passage. Mission is critical. Support to Cairo.*

She looked up from the paper at the man smiling.

"So, you know that..."

"Yes."

"Which means you must be…"

"Yes."

She smiled, and started to relax.

"What am I to call you?"

"Call me Liam."

As the waiter returned with the man's tea, Charlotte tucked the note into her handbag. *Who else knew she had come to Egypt?* She wondered. Another piece for the puzzle.

"Miss Cook, you are not safe."

"I am aware. What more do you know?"

"We received this message from London yesterday. We followed you from the dock to the train station. We have the situation under control."

"We?"

"Yes, *we*. I believe you spotted both Patrick and I in the hallway earlier?"

"Yes, I did," she blushed. The two British men *had* been following her.

***

"Wait, so this guy is helping Charlotte?" I interrupted, "I totally thought he was a bad guy!"

"Me too," Little Finn piped in.

"Any other questions?" Grandpa asked.

None of us had any, so grandpa kept reading.

***

After Charlotte finished her toast and coffee, and Liam finished his tea, the two of them stood from the table. Liam offered to walk Charlotte back to her room, and Charlotte accepted. *Better safe than sorry*, she thought.

Liam explained that Patrick would be waiting for them outside her room, guarding her belongings.

When the two of them entered Car 4, they heard shouting. A door swung open - Charlotte's door - and a tall, thin man stepped out. Was it the same man she had passed earlier? The one who smelled like coffee?

Before she could get a good look, he darted down the hall in the opposite direction. Liam chased after him.

Charlotte didn't know what to do, so she followed. As she passed her room, she saw a British man lying on the floor. *Was it Patrick?* She saw her suitcase dumped and her clothes spread around the room.

She looked down the hall. Liam and the other man were already in the next car. Liam was right. Charlotte wasn't safe.

# 5

## Dr. Amenti

Quickly, Dr. Bell shoved her belongings back into her suitcase, and left Room 6/7. Heading back toward the restaurant car, Charlotte spotted an empty room in Car 3. She slipped inside the room and quickly locked the door behind her.

Slumping on the couch of the empty room, Charlotte took a deep breath and tried to relax. She stared out the window at the changing landscape, thinking. She could see Cairo in the distance.

Charlotte listened carefully for footsteps in the corridor outside her room.

Nothing.

She took another breath, and let it out slowly. Then, she pulled Liam's telegram from her handbag and read it again. She wondered about Liam, and Patrick, and the tall, thin man.

Charlotte sat awake and alert on the couch of that empty room in Car 3 for the rest of the journey.

She had locked the door and closed the curtains. Every footstep in the hallway, every passenger talking outside the door, reminded her of the dangers ahead. There she sat, thinking. She held her notebook tightly for over an hour, as the train completed its journey to Cairo.

She needed to be more careful.

Charlotte opened the leather cover of her notebook and took out a newspaper clipping - an

48

advertisement for the Egyptian Museum. It had opened just over twenty years ago, in 1902, and had the most extensive collection of Ancient Egyptian artifacts in the world.

She hoped the museum had answers to some of her questions. Before leaving England, Dr. Bell had arranged an appointment with *the* Dr. Amenti, a world-famous archeologist in charge of Egypt's antiquities. He practically ran the museum. Undoubtedly, he could help.

At last, the train slowed, and jerked to a halt at Ramses Station, in the center of Cairo.

Charlotte slipped into a new outfit to throw off anyone trying to follow her, and waited until the train emptied. She waited, and waited, and waited.

Once all the passengers were gone, and train attendants were busy cleaning the rooms, Dr. Charlotte Bell slipped out of the back of Car 3 wearing tan pants and a white blouse. She tucked her long hair inside a wide brimmed leather hat, picked up her bags, and quickly disappeared into the crowded station.

***

"Oo-oo-oo!" Finn blurted out. "This is getting exciting!"

"Indeed," grandpa smiled, lifting his eyes and sliding down his glasses to look at each of us.

"I'm a little nervous, grandpa," Sissie spoke up. "What happened to that tall man who smells like coffee?"

"Yeah," I chimed in, "and what about Liam and Patrick? Aren't they supposed to protect her?"

"I guess we'll have to wait and see," grandpa answered.

He adjusted his glasses, turned back to the book, and continued reading.

"Now, where were we?"

\*\*\*

Charlotte arrived at the street, quickly hailed a taxicab, and ducked into the back seat.

"Egyptian Museum, please," she said nervously, without looking at the driver.

Her eyes scanned the train station crowds - watching carefully for the tall man, Liam, or Patrick.

"Of course, madam," the driver replied.

As her taxi pulled away, she spotted Liam and Patrick through the rear window. They raced out of the train station, and into the street, pointing and shouting frantically. There was no sign of the tall man. She tried to relax.

The taxi carried her a long way down a wide road. Ahead, she could see bridges and barges - they were nearing the Nile River. As they closed in on the river, she spotted the museum, rising on her right - a large red building that looked more like an old palace than a museum. The sun burned hot, high in the sky.

Dr. Bell gathered her things, paid the driver, and headed inside.

The Egyptian Museum rested along the Nile River. Charlotte walked up the stone steps and through the grand doors into an enormous entry hall. A gentle breeze pulled air through large open windows at either end of the main hall.

Dr. Bell took a slow deep breath, and let herself smile. She tried to forget the dangers of the train. She had waited nearly her whole life to see the treasures in this building. Charlotte walked up to a large wooden desk near the entrance.

"Hello, I'm here to speak with Dr. Amenti?"

The receptionist, an older English woman in a dark floral dress, looked up from her books.

"Zil?"

"Yes," Charlotte repeated herself, "Dr. Zil Amenti."

"Wonderful, you must be Miss Cook?" the woman stood and offered a handshake, "My name is Violet."

Charlotte shook Violet's hand and smiled, "Pleasure to meet you, Violet."

Violet smiled back, "Zil is working on the second floor, studying some of the newest remains found in the Valley of the Kings. Your bags will be safe here, and I will take you to him."

Charlotte set her suitcase and handbag down behind the reception desk, keeping only her notebook with her as they walked. She followed Violet up a grand staircase to the second floor. From there, Violet led Dr. Bell across a large exhibit hall to locked door. Behind it was a narrow hallway.

Doors to offices and workrooms lined the hall. Behind each door, scientists worked busily, restoring all kinds of ancient artifacts. Charlotte couldn't help but peek into the small window on each door.

"This way, dearie," Violet tugged Charlotte ahead. "We mustn't keep Zil waiting."

Violet headed into a door near the end of the hall. Charlotte followed. Thick metal shelving lined the walls, and each shelf held an assortment of rare artifacts - masks, staffs, papyrus scrolls, smooth rocks covered in hieroglyphs, pottery, instruments, and jewelry including a few crowns.

In the center of the room, a number of scientists in white lab coats stood over a large metal table. Charlotte's heart skipped a beat when she realized what the table held - a real-life mummy, cloth wrapped and dusty.

*Incredible*, she thought.

When the door shut behind Charlotte, the scientists all looked up.

"Miss Cook?" asked one of the scientists, a handsome Egyptian man carrying a clipboard.

"Yes," Charlotte replied.

"Excellent," he said. He stepped away from the table and greeted her with a firm handshake. "I am Dr. Amenti. Please, you will call me Zil."

"Yes, of course," Charlotte answered nervously as she shook his hand.

Looking past Dr. Amenti, to the mummy on the table, she added, "Is that *him*?"

"It is," he responded calmly, "Now, follow me.

# 6

## The Forgotten Pharaoh

For the next several hours, Zil led Charlotte on an extensive tour of the museum. At each exhibit, Charlotte asked more questions. Dr. Amenti answered with many stories, painting a beautiful picture of Ancient Egypt.

He also paid close attention whenever Miss Cook opened her notebook.

She checked her notebook frequently during the tour, occasionally adding new notes to various pages, and comparing her notebook sketches to the Egyptian artifacts on display.

All in all, it was a wonderful afternoon. Now, as they stood in front of a brightly decorated gold mask, Charlotte busily jotted notes in her leather book.

"Miss Cook," Dr. Amenti observed, "you seem particularly interested in the Valley of the Kings."

"Yes," she answered, only half paying attention.

Dr. Amenti stepped closer.

"Perhaps the tomb of the Forgotten Pharaoh interests you?" he added in a whisper, peeking over her shoulder and into her notebook.

Charlotte froze for a moment, and looked up.

"So, I've figured it out?" Dr. Amenti smiled, "It makes perfect sense. Ever since you sent that first telegram, asking to visit our museum - to meet with me - I have hoped you were interested in the Forgotten Pharaoh."

Charlotte smiled weakly and closed her notebook.

Dr. Amenti kept whispering, "Am I right? Have you travelled all the way from England to learn if the legend is true?"

"Is it?" Dr. Bell whispered back.

A smile crept across his face as he raised his finger to his lips.

"Follow me," he whispered. "It's not safe to speak here."

Dr. Amenti led Dr. Bell back to the second-floor offices, occasionally peeking over his shoulder to be sure they were alone. Charlotte hurried along, holding the notebook tight to her side.

They made their way through the same locked door Violet had opened earlier, and stopping halfway down the narrow hallway, Dr. Amenti unlocked an office on the right.

They both stepped inside. Dr. Amenti locked the door and pulled down the window shade.

Charlotte could feel her heart pounding in her chest.

"We can speak freely here," Dr. Amenti whispered. "Please, sit."

***

Grandpa paused reading and looked up at Finn.

"Are you okay?" he asked. "You're squirming like you have ants in your pants."

"I think I might need a bathroom break," Finn smiled.

"Go," grandpa laughed, "we can wait."

Finn giggled and ran down the hallway to the bathroom. Grandpa took the opportunity to refill his tea while Sissie and I waited at the table.

Even in the daylight, you could see the soft glow of white light lifting from the pages.

"Want to go to Egypt?" I whispered to Sissie.

"Don't even think about it!" grandpa hollered from the kitchen.

Sissie and I laughed under our breaths.

"Wouldn't it be amazing?" she whispered back.

Grandpa sat back at the table with another steaming cup of coffee just as Finn was returning with clean hands and an empty bladder.

"You two look like trouble," grandpa said with a smile, and he continued reading.

***

"Well, is it true?" Charlotte asked again, now that they were safe in Zil's office.

"I have been asking that question nearly all my life," he replied.

"And?" she insisted, leaning forward in her chair.

"And, I am still searching for the answer," Zil sighed.

Charlotte's eyes dropped, and she settled back in her seat.

After a moment of reflection, Dr. Amenti asked, "When did you first hear the legend of the Forgotten Pharaoh?"

Dr. Bell lifted her eyes, "I first heard the legend as a little girl."

All her research, all those years, led her to this moment - to *this* adventure. Finally, she could talk with someone who understood. She was certain Dr. Amenti could help.

Charlotte smiled as she remembered, "Heavy rain battered my bedroom window. Thunder shook the glass, and lightening splintered the sky. I tried to hide under my blankets. I couldn't sleep. My father came in to comfort me - to help me feel safe. When I asked him to tell me a story, he began talking about a poor boy born in the desert. The boy lived in Ancient Egypt and his life was full of incredible adventures. In the end, that poor boy grew up to be King of all Egypt. Dad's stories - the Forgotten Pharaoh - didn't just get me through the storm, they changed the course of my life."

"Yes," Zil nodded, "My father told me the same tales on many such nights."

"I loved the stories so much, I begged him to tell them - over and over." Charlotte went on, "Every detail of the stories captivated me - the streak of gray in his mother's hair, his miraculous escape from the flooding prison."

"His first encounter with the Pharaoh's daughter along the reeds of the Nile," Zil added.

"Yes," Charlotte nodded, leaning forward, "and the story *felt* real. I began to wonder if it could really be true."

Dr. Bell paused, nervously rubbing her notebook, her heart still pounding with excitement.

"And?" Zil leaned across the desk.

"Now, I *know*," she whispered.

"Know what?"

"That the legend *is* true," she whispered, as a smile took over her face.

Dr. Zil Amenti stared back in silent disbelief.

"How could you know?"

"I discovered a map."

***

"Wait, so Charlotte's like, a treasure hunter or something?" I asked.

"She might be an archaeologist," Sissie jumped in.

"Either way," I said, "she sounds super cool."

"Totally," little Finn chimed in.

"Super cool indeed," grandpa smiled. "Back to the book?"

We all nodded.

***

"A map?" he asked.

Dr. Bell smiled, "The map to his tomb."

Zil sat back in his chair, speechless. So, he *had* guessed correctly. She *did* find the map. He could feel his own heart begin to race. He had to see that map. For years he had searched, and now, this English woman discovers *his* map?

Dr. Amenti leaned forward again.

"This is why you are in Egypt?"

"Yes," she nodded.

"Well," Zil smiled, "How can I help?"

***

"I don't like that professor!" Little Finn blurted out.

Startled, grandpa looked up from the book.

"No?" grandpa asked.

"No. I don't trust him." Finn blurted again.

"Why not?" I asked. "It sounds like she went to the museum to get his help."

"Yeah," Sissie chimed in. "He knows all about the museum, and he's been looking for the Forgotten Pharaoh too."

"That's true," grandpa added. "Finn, can I keep reading?

"Yeah," he sighed reluctantly, "but I don't trust that museum guy."

7

## Liam & Patrick

Charlotte fidgeted with her notebook.

"I need to make my way south to Luxor," she replied. "I've booked passage on the steamship, SS Arabia. The journey begins this evening."

An awkward silence hung in the air.

Charlotte hesitated, then added, "Can you join me?"

Dr. Amenti glanced at the notebook, still tightly in Charlotte's grip.

"It is a generous offer, but I have important business here in Cairo tomorrow."

7

Charlotte looked away, disappointed. Without Dr. Amenti's help, the journey would be much more difficult. After all, he knew the land, language, and customs far better than she did.

"I understand," Charlotte sighed.

"Perhaps," Zil leaned forward, "perhaps, I could meet you in Luxor?"

"Yes, that would be wonderful," Charlotte smiled.

"Where will you be staying?"

"At the Sofitel Winter Palace."

"Excellent, Dr. Amenti smiled as he stood, "I will meet you there when my business in Cairo is complete. Now, if you will excuse me, I have new travel arrangements to secure."

"Yes of course," Charlotte smiled and stood.

Dr. Amenti led Charlotte out of the office. The two of them headed to Violet's desk to collect her suitcase and handbag and call a taxi. After helping Charlotte into the taxi, Dr. Amenti headed back into the museum.

"Did you and Miss Cook have a nice chat?" Violet asked with a devious smile.

Zil nodded, "Better than expected. Did you find anything?"

"Nothing interesting. She kept the notebook close."

"Indeed, she did," Dr. Amenti replied.

Violet checked her watch, "They're waiting for you in the basement."

"Excellent."

Dr. Amenti wore a devious smile of his own. Quickly, he made his way down a private staircase to a dim lit corner in the museum basement. Zil passed through a small door, into a hidden room.

"Gentlemen," Dr. Amenti said, as he entered.

There sat two tired, sweaty, well dressed Englishmen - Liam and Patrick.

***

"Wait a second," I interrupted, "Are those the guys from the train?"

Sissie looked confused too.

"The ones who tried to help Charlotte?" Little Finn asked.

"I think so," Sissie replied.

"I thought they worked for the Queen of England," I replied. "Does Dr. Amenti works for the Queen of England too?"

"No way!" little Finn announced. "I still don't trust that Dr. Amenti guy."

"Shall we keep reading?" grandpa asked.

We nodded.

***

"Yeah boss?" Liam and Patrick responded.

"What happened?"

Patrick looked down.

Liam decided to answer, "We did like you told us. We got on the train. We introduced ourselves. We delivered the note - told her we could keep her safe."

"And then?" Dr. Amenti asked impatiently.

"Then, we lost her," Patrick sighed.

"You lost her?"

Liam and Patrick looked away.

"You lost her?" Dr. Amenti said again in a slightly louder tone.

Dr. Amenti slammed his hand on the table - scaring the Englishmen so much they nearly fell out of their seats.

"This is important work!" Dr. Amenti shouted.

Liam and Patrick nodded, looking at the ground. Dr. Amenti took a long slow breath and sat down across from them. Beginning again, he spoke in a steady, calculated tone.

"As we expected, Dr. Bell is heading to the Valley of the Kings."

Liam took out a small notebook and started writing: *Valley of the Kings.*

Patrick kept nodding.

"Dr. Bell is still traveling under a false name - Miss Charlotte Cook."

Liam wrote in the notebook: *Miss Cook.* Then, he thought for a moment.

"But, we know her real name, right? It's Dr. Bell."

"Yes Liam," Dr. Amenti spoke patiently, "We know her real name is Dr. Bell."

"And," Liam continued, "*she* knows *we* know her real name, because of the note *we* gave her on the train, right?

"Yes Liam, *she* knows *you* know her real name."

"What about you, boss?" Patrick asked.

"No. She doesn't know that I know her real name."

Patrick nodded.

Liam added to his notebook: *She knows we know, but not that he knows.*

"And," Dr. Amenti went on, "she still thinks you two were sent from the British government to protect her, right?"

Liam grunted, "Uh-huh."

Patrick kept nodding.

"So, what's the plan boss?" Liam asked.

"I have business here tomorrow," Dr. Amenti said. "I need the two of you on that steam ship. You know what to do. Finish the job."

"Got it boss," Liam said, as he added to his notebook: *On steam ship, finish the job.*

"Violet will make the arrangements," Dr. Amenti went on. "You'll board this evening, and I'll catch up with you in Luxor. Charlotte expects me to meet her at the Sofitel Winter Palace."

Liam jotted in his notebook: *Luxor, Winter Palace. Meet Dr. Amenti.*

"You two will meet me there," Dr. Amenti continued. "Violet has a room arranged for you two - Room 114."

Liam nodded while he wrote: *Room 114.*

"Do you think you can finish the job?"

Liam grunted again, "Yeah boss."

Patrick tilted his head, like a confused puppy.

"Did you tell her about us?" he asked.

"Of course not," Dr. Amenti snapped. "That would ruin everything."

\*\*\*

"What did he mean by that?" Sissie asked.

"I have no idea," I said, "but now *I* have to pee like crazy."

"Me too!" little Finn shouted as he raced to the bathroom.

"Again? You just went!" I asked, chasing Finn down the hall.

Grandpa and Sissie laughed. In a few minutes we were back at the kitchen table, ready to hear more of the story.

"Well," grandpa asked, "How do you like the adventure so far?"

"I don't like it," little Finn smiled wide, "I love it, grandpa!"

"Us too," Sissie and I said, "Keep reading!"

"Alright, alright!"

Grandpa smiled, turned the page, and continued to read.

# 8
## SS Arabia

Across the Nile from the Egyptian Museum, Charlotte settled into her cabin aboard the SS Arabia - a luxurious three-story steamship that would transport her to Luxor. Her private room had a large bed covered in gold and purple furnishings. The windows wore long purple curtains with gold stitching. Charlotte stepped in and locked the door behind her. She set her luggage and handbag down next to an antique desk decorated with a small oil lamp, some paper, and a fountain pen.

Charlotte tugged a small model steamship from the bottom of her handbag and sat down on the large bed. She ran her fingers across the worn toy - a gift from her father so many years ago. Ever since she had opened that gift - since she heard his stories about *this* place, about *this* journey - she dreamed of sailing the Nile.

Now, her dream was becoming reality. In two weeks, she would be in Luxor.

Her father would be proud of his adventuring princess. That's what he had called her, *My Adventuring Princess*. She laid back in the bed and threw her arms wide. Thinking of her father made her happy.

Thick, humid air and market spices drifted into the room on a light warm breeze. Charlotte began to relax for the first time since arriving in Egypt.

She remembered all that had happened. What a day it had been: the overnight train, the museum, the mummy, Dr. Amenti, and now, aboard the SS Arabia. Her eyes grew heavy.

*I've got some time before dinner*, she thought. *A short nap wouldn't hurt.*

Charlotte fell asleep easily, drifting into a dream with the rock of the boat. The toy steamship slipped out of her hand. It seemed to float on the ocean of purple and gold blankets.

***

"Charlotte's really cool, grandpa!" Sissie announced.

"I agree," I added.

"This story is awesome," little Finn chimed in. "Can we keep reading?"

"Absolutely," grandpa said, and he kept reading.

***

Quiet whispering interrupted Charlotte's sleep. Startled, she listened.

The doorknob jostled.

"Hello?" she called from the bed, still half asleep.

More whispering, footsteps leaving, then silence.

Charlotte sat up, groggy and confused. The room had grown much darker while she napped. As evening overtook day, a deep blue sky replaced the bright afternoon sun. A cool breeze, ruffled past the purple curtains.

Suspicious, Charlotte tiptoed to the door. Holding her breath, she listened. Nothing.

*Probably just someone visiting the wrong room*, she thought.

***

"Who do you think was at the door?" I asked, interrupting the story.

"That museum guy?" little Finn offered.

"I think it was those two guys from England," Sissie chimed.

"Liam and Patrick?" I asked.

"Yep," she smiled. "Probably checking to make sure Charlotte was safe."

Finn and I exchanged glances - I don't think either of us trusted those British guys. I started to wonder if anyone in the story really wanted to help Dr. Bell.

"You know," I said, "they don't really work the Queen."

Sissie rolled her eyes at me.

"May I continue reading?" grandpa asked patiently.

We all nodded, and he continued.

***

Charlotte hadn't realized how exhausted she was from the trip so far. She walked to the window and stretched her arms. The SS Arabia had started its long journey down the Nile, and Cairo's evening lights flickered in the distance.

She stretched and yawned, taking in the soft warm breeze. Mid-stretch Charlotte's stomach growled. Between the exciting train ride that morning, and exploring the museum most of the day, she had forgotten to eat.

*The dining room should be open*, she thought.

Charlotte grabbed her handbag and room key, and headed out.

In the hall, Charlotte passed other guests - a French couple on vacation, several Americans who looked like researchers, a group of British men discussing politics in Egypt.

Turning the corner, a tall man with dark hair bumped into her, knocking her handbag to the deck. He pressed past her quickly, hiding his face and not saying a word.

*How rude*, she thought, as she knelt down to collect her handbag.

Then, she smelled it - the scent of strong coffee.

***

Grandpa took another long pause from reading.

"It's that tall, thin man again, isn't it?" Sissie asked.

Grandpa nodded, "Yes."

"Do you remember him yet?" I asked.

"No," grandpa answered without looking up.

He paused for another moment, and then continued reading.

***

*Was that the man from the train?* She wondered. She hadn't seen his face.

Charlotte took a quick peek around the corner, trying to get a second look at him, but the tall man who smelled like coffee was gone.

Gathering herself, Charlotte headed toward the dining room, anxious for a meal. Passing several seated guests, she settled at an empty table near the kitchen with a large window view.

Charlotte took one of the two seats facing the main entrance, with her back to the kitchen. She placed her handbag on the seat next to her, against the window, and paused to take in the view. Large, open windows offered sweeping landscapes along either bank of the Nile. A hum of quiet conversation and light music from a phonograph filled the dining room with life and stories.

A waiter leaving the kitchen approached her table.

"Good evening," he smiled, "May I start you with mint tea this evening?"

"Yes, please." Charlotte replied.

"Here is the menu," he smiled, "I'll return shortly with the tea."

"Thank you," Charlotte smiled.

As he left, Charlotte spotted Liam at the dining room entrance. He spotted her, too, and walked casually to her table.

"Evening Miss Cook," Liam smiled, "Are these empty seats saved?

Before Charlotte could answer, he settled into the seat directly across from her.

Liam and Charlotte exchanged pleasantries - small talk like *hello, how are you, fine weather this evening*. The waiter stopped at the table again and took their orders - though he had forgotten Charlotte's tea.

When the waiter had finished, Charlotte looked Liam square in the eyes and asked, "What are you doing on the SS Arabia?"

"I could ask you the same thing," Liam smiled, "You really gave us the slip back at the train station."

"Yes, sorry," Charlotte spoke while looking out the window, still unsure who to trust.

"Did you enjoy Cairo?" Liam asked.

"I did," she replied.

Then, she spotted Patrick at the dining room entrance. He made his way to their table and sat down next to Liam - across from the handbag.

"It's not there," Patrick spoke in husky whisper.

## 9

## Overboard

"What do you mean it's not there?" Liam asked with a heavy London accent.

"I checked everywhere."

"You sure?" Liam asked again.

"Aye mate," Patrick said, turning to Charlotte, "She must have it on her."

Then, Patrick added, "I did find *this*," lifting a small toy steamship from his pocket and placing on the table.

Charlotte's heart began to race.

Both men looked back at Charlotte with crooked smiles.

"Dr. Bell," Liam said, pausing to crack his knuckles, "we don't want anyone to get hurt, but we need to take a peek in that handbag of yours."

Charlotte tightened her grip on the bag. She tried to remain calm. Her heart pounded inside her chest.

Patrick leaned forward with a menacing smile, and placed his elbows on the table.

"It seems you have something important," he continued. "We've been sent to collect it."

*Did they know about her notebook?* She didn't budge.

"I thought you were sent to help me," Charlotte whispered, "the letter from the Queen?"

"Yeah, well, that may not have been completely honest of us," Patrick laughed revealing several missing teeth.

Charlotte looked at the steamship on the table. She thought of her father - she always felt brave when she thought of him.

"Now, Miss Charlotte," Liam whispered, "don't make a scene. Just pass *it* under the table quietly and we can all get on with our evenings."

Charlotte drew in a deep breath, looked Liam square in the eyes, and said, "No."

"What?" Patrick tilted his head, confused.

"No," she repeated. "You'll have to take it from me."

Patrick may have been confused, but Liam understood perfectly. He jumped to his feet, reached across the table, and grabbed Charlotte's arm, lifting her from her seat.

Leaning close, Liam whispered, "Don't make a scene. It'll only make things worse."

\*\*\*

"Grandpa!" Sissie interrupted. "This is crazy!"

"I knew those guys were bad news," Finn grumbled.

Then, I jumped in, "We've got to do something!"

"What do you propose? Grandpa asked.

"I don't know," Sissie insisted, "something!"

I tried to think. There wasn't much we could do. If we sent a note, Liam and Patrick would see it. If we flashed in, we'd be in trouble too.

"Maybe we should read a little further," I suggested.

Little Finn nodded, "She's the hero, right? We'll have a chance to help her later, when it's safe."

"Fine," Sissie complained, "But I *so* don't like those British guys."

We all laughed a little, and asked grandpa to keep reading.

***

Charlotte glanced to the left and right. Several passengers dining at the other tables had noticed the commotion. They were beginning to stare.

Just then, the kitchen door swung open. The waiter had remembered Charlotte's tea. Surprised to see guests standing in his path, the waiter tripped over Liam - spilling boiling water across his chest.

"Ooowww!" he howled, letting go of Charlotte's arm.

Realizing her fortune, Charlotte ran.

Patrick followed.

Charlotte raced out back of the restaurant into the kitchen, holding her handbag tight. She turned left, then right, passing chefs and food storage.

Desperate to protect the notebook, Charlotte slid her handbag behind a stack of pomegranate boxes. After a few more turns, she was outside again.

She hurried along the dark, narrow walk toward the back deck. A few steps later, she heard Patrick burst out of the kitchen, his footsteps gaining on her.

If she could just reach the back deck, maybe someone would see her. Someone could help.

She ran hard, looking over her shoulder. Patrick was closing in.

Then a door swung open right in front of her.

"Thud!"

She ran right into Liam.

"Well hello there, Dr. Bell," he chuckled, grabbing her by the hands and holding her tight.

Patrick caught up, out of breath.

"Where is it?" Patrick wheezed, out of breath from the run. "Where's the notebook?"

"You can't have it," Charlotte screamed, kicking hard against Liam.

"Easy, doc," Liam said sternly. "We're getting that notebook one way or another."

"Never," she screamed again, still kicking.

Swinging her feet forward, Charlotte kicked at Patrick. One foot caught him just under the chin, knocking him off-balance. Charlotte watched him swing backwards over the rail.

"Help!" Patrick hollered, as he fell. One of his hands grabbed hold of the rail.

"What's the matter with you," Liam shouted at Patrick.

"I didn't try to fall," Patrick whimpered back, holding tight to the rail.

"Stop foolin' around and help me with the girl!" Liam hollered back. "There's crocs in that water!"

Liam tried to get closer to the railing, still holding Charlotte – her legs swinging violently in the air.

"Hang on, Patrick," Liam sighed, "I'm coming for you."

He tried to hold Charlotte with one arm so he could reach Patrick with the other.

Charlotte kept kicking - her head now hanging over the rail, her feet still swinging.

"Liam, I can't hold on much longer," Patrick whined.

Charlotte, now upside down, managed to get one arm free of Liam. She grabbed on to the lower rail.

"Hold on, Patrick," Liam hollered back.

Charlotte heard new footsteps. Someone else was on the deck.

"This is none of your concern," Liam bellowed at the footsteps.

Liam sounded angry, and a little scared.

"Liam!" Patrick yelled up from the rail.

"Hold on..."

"Splash!" Patrick belly flopped into the Nile!

"Liam, help!" he hollered again, bobbing up and down in the river. "The crocs!"

Charlotte felt herself slipping. She tried to hook one of her legs onto the upper rail.

"Patrick, no!" Liam shouted toward the water.

He dropped Charlotte, and turned to face the stranger on deck.

When Patrick let go of Charlotte, her feet slipped off the rail and swing low. Straining, she grabbed hold of the rail with both hands.

Her heart raced. Her feet danced on atop the cool Nile water.

For the moment, she was safe – even if her toes were a little wet – but, how long could she hold on?

Overhead, she heard a scuffle. Two men talking, fighting. Punches flew. Suddenly, she watched Liam roll over the rail and dropped past her into the river.

"Splash!"

Charlotte looked across the dark river. As the boat sailed on, Liam and Patrick bobbed behind. She could hear Liam, splashing and calling for Patrick.

Charlotte looked up. A tall man stepped to the rail. She couldn't see him in the dark - only his silhouette - but she smelled coffee.

Then, he disappeared.

"Help!" she screamed. "I can't hold on forever!"

Nothing.

Her hands ached. They were slipping. She thought of the crocodiles.

"Help!" she screamed again.

She heard footsteps. A few new silhouettes leaned over the rail.

"Hello?" voices called down to her.

"Help, please!" Charlotte called up.

Then, a few more silhouettes. Passengers gathering to help.

One lowered a buoy to her. Several others helped lift her to the deck. Another wrapped her in a towel.

She was a mess - soaked and missing shoes. She thanked the passengers who helped her, and hurried to the steamship's kitchen. She needed to retrieve her handbag.

Charlotte snuck back into the storage area and reached behind the pomegranate boxes.

Nothing. She reached again. Still nothing.

Her bag was gone. She began to worry.

Charlotte hurried into the dining room to retrieve the toy steamship.

It wasn't there either. Not on the table. Not under the table.

Hair still dripping, she hung her head, discouraged. No notebook – what would she do? *I'll never find the tomb without my map*, she thought, tears welling up.

Slowly, she turned toward her room. At least Liam and Patrick were gone. Perhaps changing into dry clothes would lift her spirits.

When she opened the door, her face lit up.

Sitting on the bed, she saw her handbag and toy steamship.

But how?

She shut and locked the door behind her and hurried to the bed - to the handbag.

*Her notebook? Was it there?*

Tucked safely inside the handbag, she found it, just as she had left it.

*But how?* she wondered.

# 10

## Winter Palace

From that moment until the boat docked in Luxor, Charlotte actually enjoyed her journey on the SS Arabia. The food tasted great and the sights took her breath away. Best of all, she didn't have to see or think about Liam and Patrick.

She also didn't see the tall man who smelled like coffee.

Instead, for thirteen wonderful days, she savored the peaceful adventure. All that was about to end. The SS Arabia had nearly arrived in Luxor.

Stretched out on her soft bed, looking up at the wood paneled ceiling, Charlotte began to think about her meeting with Dr. Amenti.

*** 

"Grandpa," Sissie interrupted, "I think now's the time."

"Yeah!" Finn giggled.

"Time for what?" I asked.

"To send Charlotte a note!" Finn chimed.

The book glowed a bit.

Grandpa laughed, "I think the story agrees."

"Well," grandpa asked, "what would you like to say?"

"We should tell her that Liam and Patrick work for Dr. Amenti," Sissie announced.

Finn and I agreed.

"Go ahead, Sissie," grandpa nudged.

Sissie drew a deep breath, and spoke clearly at the book: "Be warned. Liam and Patrick work for Dr. Amenti."

The pages of the book fluttered lightly, and the pages glowed bright.

"Be warned?" I teased.

Sissie blushed.

Grandpa gave me a funny look over his glasses, "Be nice."

Then, he continued reading.

*** 

As Charlotte stared up, studying the wood paneled ceiling in her room, something strange happened. The warm Nile breeze carried a small piece of folded paper in through the window and across the bed. It landed softly on her desk.

Charlotte's eyes followed the paper as it drifted. Curious, she walked to the desk, picked up the paper, unfolded it and read:

*Be warned. Liam and Patrick work for Dr. Amenti.*

Charlotte's eyes grew large as she read the note again. Her heart raced:

*Where did this come from? Is it a clue? From who?*

She glanced out the window, but the deck was empty. Just an open view of the Nile river as they docked in Luxor.

Charlotte read the message a third time, slowly. Her mind settled on the most important question:

*Could it be true?*

She wondered.

She grabbed her purse and tugged out her notebook. She reviewed her research. How did the message fit?

A loud horn interrupted.

*Luxor? Already?* She thought.

Charlotte slipped the paper clue into her notebook, collected her things, and headed toward the dock.

It was time to face Dr. Zil Amenti.

***

"She's not still going to meet Dr. Amenti, is she?" Sissie interrupted.

"She can't!" Finn jumped in. "He's trying to steal the notebook!"

"But he *does* know his way around Egypt," I said with a smile. "Maybe she knows something we don't."

Grandpa looked up from the book, "Shall I continue?"

We nodded, *yes*.

***

The Sofitel Winter Palace was a short walk from the dock - on the edge of Luxor, facing the river. Charlotte picked up her medium sized leather suitcase and small handbag and headed to the hotel.

As Charlotte entered the lobby, Liam and Patrick carved their way through a local market on the other side of the hotel. Getting to Luxor had been challenging. After falling overboard, they had to dodge crocodiles, swim to shore, fight off locals, steal a car, and eventually stow away on a train car - all just to arrive here, in Luxor.

Their clothes had dried, but were tattered and dusty from the difficult journey. Their bellies growled for food. Their eyes hung heavy, and their feet ached. Worse than that, Dr. Amenti would be disappointed - they still didn't have the notebook.

In the thick of the market, they ducked into an alley and found the hidden door - a back entrance to the Winter Palace. The door led to a small storage room, where they paused while

Liam reviewed his still soggy notes one more time:

*Luxor, Winter Palace - back door. Meet Dr. Amenti, Room 114.*

"Right," he grunted at Patrick, "Room 114."

They passed through the storage, through the hotel laundry, and into the first-floor hallway.

*124, 122, 120, 118, 116...*

"Here," Patrick whispered, "Room 114."

They tried the door. It opened easily. They slipped inside, and prepared to face a disappointed Dr. Amenti.


One floor up, in Room 210, Charlotte placed her luggage on the dresser. Her room was cool and spacious. She walked to the room's large window and drew the curtains. The market bustled below. Charlotte slid the window open, letting the sounds and smells of Luxor reach into her room. The late afternoon sun had passed overhead, and cool shade began to stretch across the market.

A knock at the door interrupted her.

"Hello?" she called over the sounds of the market.

"Miss Cook?"

She recognized Zil's voice. Her heart began to race.

"Yes," she answered in a steady voice.

"Miss Cook," the voice repeated, "are you settling in?"

"Yes," she answered. "It's lovely."

"May I invite you to dinner this evening?" Dr. Amenti continued, "To discuss preparations for our journey?"

"Yes, of course," she replied, gaining confidence. "Shall we meet in an hour? In the lobby?"

"Excellent," he replied. I will see you in the lobby.

*** 

"We've got to help her!" I interrupted.

"I agree," Sissie added, "Liam and Patrick are back."

"And, Dr. Amenti," little Finn jumped in.

"Right," Sissie nodded, "and Dr. Amenti. The three of them *totally* out number her."

"Well," grandpa asked, "what would you like to do?"

"Can I jump in?" Finn asked.

"I'm not sure you're ready for that, little one," grandpa smiled. "But, what would you do *if you did* jump in?"

"I'd go find Liam and Patrick and teach them a lesson!" Finn hollered, swinging his arms like a boxer.

We all started laughing.

"What if we send her another note?" Sissie asked.

The soft glow of the book got a bit brighter.

"Yeah," I joined in, "We can tell her Liam and Patrick are back."

"And that she's not alone," Finn added.

"But she is alone," Sissie said with a puzzled expression on her face.

"Nah," Finn said, starting to swing like a boxer again, "We've got her back!"

The book brightened a bit more.

"Well," grandpa thought out loud, "the book seems to like this idea. Sissie, will you do the honors? Will you send another note to Charlotte?"

"You bet," she smiled. Then, in her best adult voice, she said, "Beware! Liam and Patrick have returned, but you are not alone."

The book flashed bright.

Grandpa looked down at the book, then back at us.

Sissie, Finn and I waited anxiously.

"You three want to grab lunch?" he asked.

"Grandpa." we whined.

"Quick bathroom break?

"Grandpa."

"Can I refill my tea?" He asked, laughing.

"Grandpa!" we whined louder. He was *so* messing with us.

"Alright, alright," he smiled. "I'll keep reading."

## 11

## Layla

As Charlotte listened to Dr. Amenti's footsteps fade, the warm Nile breeze blew a small piece of paper past her. She watched it land gently on the bed.

*Could it be another clue?* She wondered, her eyes flickering with curiosity.

Charlotte hurried to the bed and unfolded the small piece of worn paper:

> *Beware! Liam and Patrick have returned, but you are not alone.*

The next hour passed quickly. Charlotte studied the note, reviewed her research, and carefully placed this clue next to the last. This adventure grew larger every moment. Her father would be proud.

Too soon, it was time to meet Zil. Charlotte picked up her notebook, not wanting to leave it in the room, and her toy steamship for good luck. Stepping into the hallway, she noticed the strong smell of Turkish coffee. She glanced up and down the hallway. It was empty. She locked her door and headed downstairs to the hotel lobby.

Zil greeted her with open arms and a wide smile.

"Welcome to Luxor," he smiled.

"Thank you Dr. Amenti," she offered. "This has been a beautiful adventure."

"Excellent," he smiled. "There is a small café close. We can eat there and discuss our plans."

Charlotte nodded. Zil led her out of the hotel and into the market. The sounds and smells overwhelmed and excited her: the meats, spices, clothes, jewelry, and voices bartering back and forth, arguing over prices.

When they arrived at the café, Zil chose a small outside table facing the market. Charlotte scanned the market. From her seat, she could see the back of her hotel. The sun had travelled behind it, shading much of the market. Charlotte could even see her open window on the second floor.

Zil sat across from her and ordered several small dishes for them to share. The waiter hurried away as the two scientists talked about the museum. After a while, Dr. Amenti asked Charlotte about her cruise. She shared carefully, leaving out everything about Liam, Patrick, and the mysterious notes that had found her.

After a while, the waiter returned with drinks and Zil turned the conversation to more pressing matters.

"Shall we discuss our plans?" he asked after sip of tea.

"Yes, of course," Charlotte replied.

"I've taken the liberty of gathering some supplies," he went on, "and I've hired a guide for the journey. I hope you don't mind."

Charlotte faked a smile. *He hired a guide without me?* she thought.

"Of course, I don't mind," she replied, trying to hide her distrust.

Dr. Amenti pulled a folded paper from his coat pocket as he spoke, and spread it out on the table. It was an old map of Egypt.

"Tonight, we are here, in Luxor," He paused, pointing at the paper.

Charlotte nodded.

"Tomorrow, we will journey to the Valley of the Kings," he continued, sliding his finger along a dotted line.

She nodded again.

"Somewhere near here," he said, lowering his voice to a whisper, "we can begin searching for the entrance to the tomb of the Forgotten Pharaoh."

"I can help with that," Charlotte whispered back, raising her notebook onto the table.

"Excellent," Dr. Amenti smiled. "Then the adventure begins in the morning."

As Amenti spoke, the waiter arrived with a tray full of small plates - each offering a unique and enticing smell. As he set the plates down, a strange flash of red light from somewhere across the market distracted Charlotte.

\*\*\*

Grandpa paused reading for a moment.

"That wasn't, you know, a flash, was it?" Sissie asked.

I wondered the same thing. Grandpa glanced at us over the book, silent.

*Red*, I thought, *red flash. That can't be good.*

All of us stared at each other in that silent moment.

"Keep reading!" Finn jumped in with a smile to change the mood. "Let's find out."

We all laughed a bit and started breathing again. Grandpa continued to read.

\*\*\*

...a strange flash of red light from somewhere across the market distracted Charlotte.

*What was that?* She thought. Charlotte stood for a moment, peering into the twilight.

Nothing.

Zil didn't seem to notice, and the exotic smells of dinner began to tickle Charlotte's nose. Realizing she hadn't eaten since the cruise,

Charlotte sat and filled her plate. Each bite tantalized her tongue with flavors.

Between bites, Charlotte asked, "When will I meet this guide you've hired?"

"I invited her to join us for dinner," Dr. Amenti smiled. "She must be running late."

Glancing at Charlotte's notebook, he added, "Before she arrives, shall we take a look at your research?"

Charlotte slid her hand over the notebook cautiously, "Of course, what would you like to discuss."

"Legend suggests there are several tests waiting for those who visit the Forgotten Pharaoh."

"Yes, I'm familiar with those stories," Charlotte replied.

"What have you found?" Zil leaned close to the table.

It was a fair question. Once in the desert, they would have limited supplies, limited water, and limited access to help. Charlotte knew better than to trust Zil, but she also needed his help.

"The best I can tell, the stories about the tomb match stories about the Forgotten Pharaoh - stories remembering how he ruled."

"Yes, that makes perfect sense," Zil pressed. "Have you found anything specific?"

She started to open the notebook, but a stranger approached the table. Charlotte paused, and Zil stood up.

"Our guest has arrived," he said. "Miss Cook, meet our guide, Layla."

"Pleased," Charlotte stood, hiding the notebook behind her back, and shook Layla's hand.

Layla wore a long, dark burgundy cloak that covered her arms and stretched to the ground. Her face and hair were covered in a dark scarf.

120

Only her blue-green eyes and black eyebrows were visible. She stood slightly shorter than Charlotte.

Layla's arrival put an end to Dr. Amenti's questions - for now - and the three of them enjoyed their meal together. They spent much of the time discussing details for the morning. Zil had arranged for camels, Layla had prepared food and supplies. Charlotte would meet them early in the hotel. They would enjoy breakfast at a nearby café, and then head into the desert.

Exhausted, Charlotte excused herself from the table and thanked Dr. Amenti for the generous dinner. As she hurried across the empty market, she thought she caught another sniff of strong coffee. She clutched her notebook tight.

Crossing the market, she glanced up at her hotel window - unfamiliar shadows flickered in the light of the room. Her heart and pace quickened.

Back at the table, Zil and Layla lingered.

"Is everything going according to plan?" Layla asked.

"Yes."

"And the thieves?"

"They are waiting for us in my room," Zil replied.

"Do they know about me?"

"Not yet."

"Well," Layla said with a dark smile, "what are we waiting for?"

The two of them stood, and headed back to the hotel - to Room 114.

\*\*\*

"Wait, what?" I interrupted.

"What what?" Grandpa asked.

"It sounds like Dr. Amenti already knows Layla," I said.

"Yeah," Sissie added, "Is she in on some plan with him?"

Grandpa smiled as we tried to sort things out.

I wondered if it had something to do with the red flash.

"Oh man," Finn jumped in, "Charlotte's really gonna need our help."

The book glowed a bit brighter.

# 12

## Clues

"Grandpa, this isn't good," Finn continued.

"Go on," Grandpa replied.

"Charlotte's all alone."

"Plus, she saw shadows in her room," I jumped in, "And, I think that tall guy who smells like coffee is still following her."

"Well," Grandpa paused, setting the book down for a moment, "what would you like to do?"

"I think it's time," I said.

"Time for what?" grandpa asked, trying to hide a smile.

"Time to visit Charlotte," Sissie answered.

"Alright," grandpa offered, "What's the plan?"

"Can I go?" Finn begged.

"Not yet," grandpa said.

Sissie and I exchanged glances. Then, she broke the silence.

"What if I flash into the hotel? I can still get there before she reaches her room.

The book flashed bright. It seemed to like Sissie's idea.

Grandpa smiled, "Alright, remember, stay safe, help Charlotte, and then come back. We don't want anything like last night happening again."

I dropped my head a little. Thinking about last night still stung.

Sissie squeezed my hand, then stood, ready to slip into the pages of the story.

"Are you sure I can't go?" Finn begged again.

"Not yet, little one," grandpa smiled and ruffled Finn's hair. "Soon you'll be ready."

Finn and I looked toward Sissie and whispered, "Good luck!"

"Thanks!" she said as her fingers met the glowing pages.

Sissie closed her eyes and pictured the hotel, just outside Charlotte's room. A white light shot up around her body and in an instant, she was sucked into the story.

"Good luck," grandpa whispered as she vanished from the room.

***

Charlotte hurried through the lobby, bracing herself for trouble. She headed up the stairs and into the hall when another flash of light startled her. This time the flash looked bright white, and it was much closer - right in front of her room.

Charlotte froze.

A young girl walked toward her out of the flash.

*What is happening?* Charlotte wondered. She tried to steady her hands. Her knees trembled.

The girl walked toward her, smiling.

"Don't be afraid. I'm here to help you Charlotte," Sissie said, "My name is Elizabeth."

Charlotte steadied herself, unsure whether this stranger could be trusted.

Sissie moved closer to Charlotte, "You can trust me."

"How can I be sure?" Charlotte asked, her voice shaking.

"I know about your journey - from the RMS Homeric, to the train ride, to the SS Arabia, and now here. I know about Patrick and Liam, and the tall man who smells like coffee."

"But how?"

"It's a long story."

Sissie giggled at the thought of telling a long story inside another story.

"I can fill you in later," Sissie continued. "Right now, I need to keep you safe. You saw shadows in your room?"

*Wow, she does know a lot*, Charlotte thought.

"Yes, I think Liam and Patrick are looking for this," she said, holding her notebook.

"Sounds likely," Sissie replied. "Shall we scare them away?"

Feeling brave, Charlotte and Elizabeth headed down the hall. Just as Charlotte reached for the doorknob, another bright flash of white light startled them both. It came from *inside* Charlotte's room.

***

"Thump!"

A sound somewhere in the house startled us. Grandpa stopped reading to listen. We froze.

"What was that, grandpa? Little Finn whispered.

Grandpa put his finger over his lips. We listened.

Finn and I traded glances. We heard a few birds outside and the occasional car passing through the neighborhood.

"Hmm, must have been nothing, Finn," grandpa spoke quietly.

He had a curious look on his face. Finn and I exchanged glances.

"Was it something in the basement?" I asked.

"Probably some old thing falling off a shelf," grandpa replied quickly. Then, he raised the book and leaned back in his chair.

Finn and I exchanged looks again. Was grandpa going to pretend it didn't happen?

"Where were we?" he mumbled to himself. "Ah, yes, here."

\*\*\*

Charlotte stepped back, but Sissie grabbed the doorknob, spun it, and pushed into the room.

Empty. Charlotte stepped in too, and shut the door behind her, turning the lock. The window curtains waved softly in the light breeze. Dim light pushed shadows to the edges. Charlotte's things strewn about across the floor. The whole room smelled a bit like coffee.

"What's going on!" Charlotte demanded, looking to Sissie for answers.

Sissie didn't know where to start. She expected to see the room a mess - it was. She expected to find Patrick and Liam rummaging through Charlotte's things - did they escape out the window? Why did it smell like coffee? Had the tall man been here? And, why had they seen a second white flash?

She looked up at the ceiling - half hoping to see a note floating down. Nothing.

"I," Sissie sighed, feeling a little helpless. "I don't know, Dr. Bell."

Sissie walked to the window and looked out across the market. No sign of Liam or Patrick. If they had been here, they got away fast - and that would have been a first for Liam and Patrick. Sissie sighed as she pulled the window closed and locked it.

Charlotte walked to the bed. She inspected her things, and quickly repacked them.

*Good*, she thought, *nothing missing. What were they looking for, whoever they were?*

She glanced down at her notebook. She set it onto the bed and slumped down, frustrated and confused.

"Charlotte," Sissie whispered, sitting next to her on the bed, "Let's talk about what I do know."

There, in the quiet of the night, Sissie and Charlotte recounted their adventures - inside and outside the story - until they both fell fast asleep.

They talked about the journey ahead, and the challenges waiting for them at the tomb. They talked about Dr. Amenti and Layla - both pretending to help. Charlotte felt confident she could handle them now. The Story Keepers would help her - Elizabeth would help her.

As they told stories and made plans - as they giggled together - they began to trust each other. Though they came from different worlds, they had much in common. They were becoming friends.

Meanwhile, when Dr. Amenti and Layla arrived at Room 114, Liam and Patrick were fast asleep on the floor. Zil slammed the door to wake them. Layla lit a lamp as the groggy thieves sat up.

"Who is she boss?" Liam asked, squinting in the lamp light.

"We'll get to that in a minute," Dr. Amenti shot back angrily. "First, explain to me why Dr. Bell still has her notebook."

Patrick and Liam looked at each other nervously.

"Well?" Dr. Amenti shouted.

Liam started bumbling through all their struggles, and Patrick added details here and there. They told Zil about trying to steal the book, falling overboard, and their crazy journey to Luxor.

Zil tapped his foot impatiently, then interrupted, "What do I pay you two for? You might be the worst thieves in Egypt."

"Sorry boss," Liam and Patrick mumbled, looking at the floor.

"Never mind all that now. We are in Luxor and tomorrow is a new day."

Then, with a wicked smile, Dr. Amenti added, "Meet Layla."

"Hello boys," the Egyptian guide said, stepping forward. "Time to get your act together. Starting early tomorrow morning, we've got a treasure to steal."

## 13

## Valley of the Kings

Early the next morning, before the sun rose, Sissie and Charlotte woke. Sissie gave Charlotte a big hug, and disappeared in bright white flash.

***

Suddenly, Sissie tumbled out of the book in a flash of white light.

"That was amazing!" Sissie squealed. "She's wonderful."

"Excellent work," Grandpa smiled. "You're really getting the hang of this Story Keeping stuff."

Finn and I rolled our eyes at each other, both wishing we had jumped into the story.

"You won't believe what we learned while you were gone," Finn gloated.

"What happened?" she asked.

"That guide Layla is nasty!" Finn blurted out, excited to be the one with new information. "And, Patrick and Liam were asleep in Dr. Amenti's room, on the floor."

"So, they were never in Charlotte's room?" Sissie asked.

"Doesn't seem like it," I answered.

Grandpa listened as we tried to piece things together.

"Grandpa," Sissie asked, "Are you guys messing with me?"

"What do you mean?" Grandpa asked.

"Well, last night in the story with Vilgor, we met some other people that moved in and out of stories."

"Go on," Grandpa nodded.

"That's right," I chimed in. "That one lady flashed green."

Sissie shot me a glance for interrupting, "The Lady of the Western Wood. And, both Deacon and Lark flashed red."

"And Vilgor said you used to flash white, right grandpa?" Little Finn chimed in.

"Indeed," grandpa smiled.

"So," Sissie continued, still upset that both Finn and I interrupted, "Did one of you sneak into the story, go to Charlotte's room, and then flash back before I got here?"

Finn and I looked at each other, a little uneasy. It made perfect sense, but we hadn't gone anywhere. Neither had grandpa.

Grandpa leaned back. He didn't seem as confused.

"Well," Sissie asked. "Were you guys messing with me or not?"

"No," little Finn answered, "We didn't flash in, but that would have been super funny."

"It wasn't funny at all Finn," Sissie answered, getting a bit nervous. "If it wasn't you, who was it?"

That's when I remembered the "thump" downstairs.

I shot a glance at grandpa. He knew I knew.

He gave me a look that said, "Don't ask," so I didn't.

"Let's keep reading," I suggested.

"Really?" Finn asked.

Sissie shot me a cold look, "Whatever."

Grandpa leaned forward, found his place in the book, and continued.

***

Charlotte smiled. She felt much more confident knowing friends were watching out for her. She packed her things and headed to the hotel lobby. Layla and Dr. Amenti met her there. The three of them headed out into the warm, quiet morning.

They walked to the market and found a quaint café. Charlotte ordered a traditional British breakfast with a warm cup of Grey Earl tea. Tired from the long night with Elizabeth, Charlotte didn't talk much. Zil and Layla chatted casually about the trip.

When they finished eating, Charlotte, Zil, and Layla headed to back to the river. At the dock, they boarded a small barge which ferried them across the Nile.

On the West side of the river, they collected camels, loaded their supplies, and headed north along the river before turning west into the desert.

"How far to the Valley of the Kings?" Charlotte asked, wiping sweat from her forehead. Even in the early morning, the sun was hot.

Layla looked slightly to the north, then across to the south, "Not long, we should arrive before lunch."

Charlotte could feel her stomach twist - that *good* nervous feeling, when you realize you're both excited and a bit scared.

Behind them and closer to the river, Liam and Patrick followed. Careful to obey Dr. Amenti and stay out of sight, the two thieves spent the early morning dodging crocodiles, battling mosquitoes, and staying close enough to follow camel tracks.

In the late morning, they saw Layla, Charlotte, and Zil turn West. Patrick and Liam followed.

"Hey," Patrick asked, "Where are we supposed to meet Layla?"

"In a cave," Liam grumbled.

"Right," Patrick nodded.

After a few minutes of silence, Patrick asked, "How are we supposed to find the cave?"

Liam stopped walking and pulled out his notes from the night before.

"We follow the camel tracks until we get to the valley entrance. Then we find the bag Layla drops. We pick up the bag. We look for a large cave to the west, climb in, and wait."

"Got it," Patrick mumbled.

After more silence, Patrick spoke up again, "This job is starting to creep me out."

Liam nodded without looking up, "Me too."

*** 

"Grandpa? I interrupted.

He stopped reading and looked up.

I continued, "Should we let Charlotte know about the bag?

The book fluttered bright white.

"Yeah, yeah, let's do it!" Little Finn dove in.

"Sissie, you got this?" I asked.

Sissie smiled, then looking at the book she said, "Watch the guide."

The book flashed again, and we all smiled. Then, grandpa started reading again.

*** 

As the sun rose high overhead, a gentle desert breeze brushed hot against Charlotte's cheek.

She tugged her scarf up over her mouth and nose. Looking ahead, she noticed a small piece of paper caught in the breeze, blowing toward her.

Layla noticed too, turning her head slightly at the sight of it.

Charlotte reached for the note and read it to herself:

*Watch the guide.*

*Layla?* She wondered.

Charlotte glanced up and met eyes with the guide. Layla had been watching Charlotte. Layla saw the note. She saw Charlotte read it.

*Does she know?* Charlotte wondered, as a shiver ran through her. *No, of course not, how could she.*

Layla slowly turned her gaze back to the trail.

Charlotte tucked the note away in her pant pocket.

*Watch the guide* - the message hung in Charlotte's mind. She kept her eyes fixed on Layla.

As their camels crested a rise in the desert, the path ahead shifted. Rocky outcroppings sat scattered before them and the path began to dropped. As it lowered into the valley, their wide path narrowed.

Finally, the Valley of the Kings.

They turned left, along the valley wall. Charlotte continued to watch Layla.

They followed the path until it closed against a sandstone outcropping. Switching back, the camels continued their descent toward the valley floor. A few minutes passed, they came to another outcropping and switched back again. This pattern repeated as they continued toward the valley floor.

The temperature continued to rise. Directly overhead, the sun stood strong. More switch backs, more dust, and deeper they travelled into the valley.

All the while, Charlotte kept her eyes on Layla.

Finally, they reached bottom. Layla led them to a small pocket of shade beneath a large sandstone overhang. She turned her camel to face Charlotte and Zil.

"Welcome," she exclaimed, "to the Valley of the Kings."

"It's beautiful," Charlotte whispered, taking a moment to look across the valley.

As she looked, Layla nodded toward Dr. Amenti.

Zil, guiding his camel alongside Charlotte.

"I haven't been here since I was a small boy," he said. Then, pointing southwest, he added, "We believe the entrance lies hidden in this direction."

As Zil spoke, Layla carefully untied a small bag and let it drop from her camel's side. It landed with a soft "Thump" next to the rock outcropping.

"Excellent," Charlotte smiled, "What are we waiting for?"

She followed Dr. Amenti deeper out into the valley. Glancing back, she noticed a small bag lying in the sand, and Layla peering back toward Luxor. Charlotte thought she had heard something drop.

She smiled about the note. Elizabeth was watching.

She would be safe.

# 14

## Charlotte's Map

From where they sat, the valley appeared to widen as it stretched southwest. They headed along the valley floor, passing several excavated tombs along the way.

Occasionally, tall canyons reached out of the valley to the left and right - like branches stretching out from a trunk. As midday turned to afternoon, they stayed close to the canyons to walk in shade whenever possible.

Meanwhile, the two thieves reached the valley floor. Liam sighed, exhausted. He wiped sweat from his rosy cheeks. Patrick, out of breath, stood with his hands on his knees.

"Do you see the bag?" Patrick mumbled.

"It's got to be here somewhere," Liam grumbled back.

"Water?" Patrick sighed.

"All out," Liam complained.

Working for Dr. Amenti had never been less fun. At least they still had a treasure to look forward to - if they could scare Charlotte off in time.

Liam followed the camel tracks to a second outcropping.

"Here!" he exclaimed, a bit of hope in his voice for the first time in days.

Patrick hurried over as Liam picked up the bag. He scanned the edge of the valley - no sign of Zil, Layla, or Charlotte.

"What now?" Patrick asked.

Liam reviewed his notes from the night before, "Pick up the bag, check. Look for a large cave to the west, climb in, and wait."

Patrick grabbed the back and checked inside.

"Water!"

"Maybe that guide Layla's not so bad after all," Patrick laughed, hurrying over to get a sip. "Now, where's that cave?"

"I see one," Patrick pointed. "Right there, beside those rocks."

Liam nodded, "Nice work friend. Maybe things are starting to go our way."

The two thieves hiked across the valley and up into the entrance of a shallow, dark cave. The air felt cool.

"Now we wait," Liam said.

The two thieves laid down on the cave floor and promptly fell asleep.

Some distance ahead, Zil, Layla, and Charlotte approached a tall, narrow canyon leading out of the valley to the northwest.

Dr. Amenti slid off his camel. Charlotte and Layla followed. They led their camels to shade at the base of the canyon wall. The camels sat. The travelers gathered nearby to talk.

"This is as far as my knowledge can take us," Layla began. "Archeologists have discovered the tombs of many pharaohs inside the boundary of this valley."

"Indeed," Zil added. "From this point forward, we will depend on your research Miss Cook. Which direction shall we head next?"

Charlotte pulled her notebook from her pocket and shuffled through the pages - reading from the book, then looking up at her surroundings, then back to the book.

Zil and Layla stood by, growing impatient.

"As we discussed last night," Charlotte began, "I believe the clues about the tomb match the stories we know about the Forgotten Pharaoh - stories remembering how he ruled."

"But at the museum you told me you found the map," Zil urged.

"I did."

"Where is it?" Layla insisted.

Charlotte bent to her knees and started to draw in the sand. Layla and Zil leaned in to watch.

"The Forgotten Pharaoh didn't rule like the other kings of Egypt," Charlotte continued. "That's what made him so special. It's also why later pharaohs wanted to forget him."

Zil bent down, intrigued. Layla tapped her foot, annoyed.

Charlotte gently traced two circles in the shaded sand.

"His way stood apart from the other pharaohs - so will his tomb. His way honored the people - so will his tomb."

Zil watched intently, nodding.

Charlotte began tracing lines - one connecting the circles, several others crossing this way and that. As she drew, she softly whispered:

*The place not hewn, he rests beneath stone.*
*Do you seek his tomb? Is your heart like his own?*

*From poverty to power, with love fighting fear,*
*Seek the cooling air, his body rests near.*

*Friend beware, only seek the tomb for right,*
*Forget not his heart, or you will face his might.*

*Your longing for adventure has almost found a cure,*
*Where dark retreats from light, you'll find him buried here.*

"What's that?" Zil interrupted. "What are you whispering?"

"A poem my father taught me," Charlotte smiled.

"What about these circles," Zil continued, "and the lines?"

Layla interrupted, "All this talk, and these lines, it doesn't look much like a map to me."

"Oh, but it is," Charlotte shot back with a knowing smile.

"We're here," she said, pointing at a line in the sand. "Look south through this canyon."

Zil and Layla looked down the canyon, then back at Charlotte.

"Don't you see it?" she asked.

Zil looked again. As the canyon stretched away from the valley, it narrowed, and became much rockier. Most of the sand had been blown back into the valley.

"A rocky canyon?" Layla suggested, unimpressed.

Zil's face lit up with excitement, "Your poem, the stone not hewn."

"That's right," Charlotte nodded. "We are getting close."

***

"Grandpa, this is amazing," Sissie interrupted. "She's amazing!"

"She really is," I exclaimed.

"She's still in trouble guys," Finn chimed in. "Don't forget about Liam and Patrick."

The book flashed a bit as little Finn spoke.

Grandpa set the book down, "I could use some more tea. Anyone need to use the bathroom?"

The three of us popped up and headed down the hall. We may have been reading all morning, but this adventure was just getting started.

Once we were all back, and grandpa's tea had steeped, he lifted the book and found his place.

"All set?" he asked.

We nodded and he continued to read.

*** 

Dr. Amenti and Charlotte gathered their things. Layla offered to stay with the camels while the two archeologists made their way through the canyon to find the tomb's entrance.

As soon as Zil and Charlotte were out of sight, Layla tugged the camels to their feet. She climbed onto one and held the lines for the other two. Quickly, she headed back across the valley floor, toward the cave where Patrick and Liam were supposed to be hiding.

"I hope those thick-headed thieves found the cave," she muttered under her breath.

*** 

"Grandpa," I interrupted, "We've got to stop Layla and the thieves from messing with Charlotte!"

"Yeah," Little Finn chimed in.

"What are you suggesting?" grandpa asked.

Sissie's face lit up.

"This is our chance!" she sounded excited, like she had a plan. "Now that they are separated, we can distract Layla *and* the thieves."

"Yeah, maybe we can scare them!" Little Finn blurted, giddy with excitement.

"We'll still need to get those camels back to the canyon so Charlotte can get home," I added.

"Oh, good thinking Riles," Finn smiled big. "Can I do it this time?"

"Not yet little one," grandpa chuckled. "Sissie?"

"I already got to go into this story," Sissie paused. "Riles, do you want to take this one."

"You don't have to ask me twice!" I answered. "Is that okay with you grandpa?"

"Sure," he smiled. "Be careful. You never know what surprise might be waiting for you inside a story."

"Got it," I smiled back. "See you guys soon!"

Then, I reached for the book. As the pages flashed bright white, I felt a swirling wind of light, then...

***

In a flash of bright white light, Riles found himself in a dark cave. He landed in soft sand behind a large rock. On the other side of the rock, two large, smelly, sweaty bodies snored.

It took a few minutes for his eyes to adjust, but he didn't need to see to know who snored on the other side of the rock. Riles had found Patrick and Liam.

## 15

## The Cave

"Sleeping again, I see?" a familiar voice called into the cave.

Riles popped his head up from behind the rock as Liam and Patrick jolted out of their peaceful slumber. She stood at the cave entrance. All Riles could see was her silhouette against the light outside.

"Get up, get up!" the voice hollered at the two thieves.

*It has to be Layla*, Riles thought. But he recognized the voice. *Where have I heard that voice?* He thought, but Riles couldn't remember.

Liam and Patrick hurried to their feet and sat on two rocks across the cave. Then, Layla stepped inside the cave as she yelled.

"Sleeping on the job!" her voice echoed in the cave. "Again!"

"A thousand apologies," Patrick and Liam sputtered.

Then it clicked. Riles remembered the voice. He remembered so quickly, he could hardly control himself.

He stood up tall and blurted, "Lark!"

Layla swung around, "Riles? I was wondering if I'd see you here."

In a flash of red light, she was on him. They wrestled back and forth until he threw her off with a white flash of his own.

Riles stood his ground. Lark picked herself up, brushed off the sand, and turned to face him a second time.

Patrick and Liam cowered against the edge of the cave. They had never seen flashes of light like this before.

"This is my story," she chided him. "You've no business being here."

"I've as much a right to be here as you," Riles shot back. "Why are you here, anyway? You can't possibly care about the Forgotten Pharaoh."

Lark laughed, "Of course not. I'm here to make sure that silly Charlotte goes home empty handed and Dr. Amenti controls the treasure."

"What's it to you?" Riles countered. "She's the one with the map, and he's just a lousy thief like them," he said, pointing toward Liam and Patrick.

"I do what I'm told," Lark answered with a fierce expression. "If it matters to Master Calamitous, it matters to me."

At that, she lunged toward Riles, but in a flash of white light, he disappeared. Lark landed empty handed in the shady sand.

"Good," she smirked, then looking toward the sky she yelled, "And stay out!"

Liam and Patrick huddled close together, terrified.

Lark strolled toward them, fuming.

"Take the camels. Head down the valley until you see my red scarf hanging on a rock. Follow that canyon to the tomb entrance. I will meet you there. Do you understand?"

Liam and Patrick nodded, too afraid to say a word.

"Good," she continued. "Don't screw up, or it'll be the last thing you do."

Seeing Riles had spooked Lark. She saw the note Charlotte received on the camel, but that was just a clue. Knowing they were reading was one thing. Seeing them inside her story – that was crossing the line. She had too much riding on this mission to let that white-flash-rookie Riles mess things up.

If she failed, Master Calamitous would be very disappointed. She needed to spoil this story.

In a flash of red light, she disappeared from the cave.

Liam and Patrick looked at each other, jumped to their feet, and ran to the camels.

***

I landed back in the kitchen with flash and a bump.

"It's Lark!" I hollered, out of breath and full of excitement. "Layla is Lark!"

Sissie and Little Finn laughed, "We know Riles! We were reading the story!"

"Oh, right. I forgot." I said, starting to laugh at myself.

"How'd it go?" grandpa asked.

"Better than last night," I smiled bigger. "It felt great to get back in the story."

"Good," he smiled back.

"Wait a sec," I looked at Sissie. "You had a whole dinner with Layla and didn't tell us she was really Lark?"

"That's because I've never met Lark, remember?"

"Oh, right, sorry, I forgot."

"That's alright," Sissie winked.

"You two good?" grandpa asked.

We nodded.

"Great, now what's the plan? Or, should I just keep reading?"

"I think we need to help Charlotte," Finn suggested. "Lark's pretty scary, and Charlotte doesn't know her like we do."

"Plus, Patrick and Liam will catch up to them soon," Sissie added.

"Oh, I've got an idea about that," I said, with a twinkle in my eye.

"Go on," grandpa nudged.

"Alright, so Patrick and Liam are supposed to go to the place where the canyon starts, right?"

"Uh-huh," grandpa said, starting to smile.

"And Lark's heading to the tomb?"

"Right," Sissie said with a nod.

"So," I continued, "When Liam and Patrick get to the canyon they'll be all alone. It's our best chance to chase them off."

"It's worth a try," Sissie smiled.

"Cool," Little Finn interrupted, "Can I do it?"

"Sorry, little one," grandpa chuckled.

"Grandpa," Little Finn crossed his arms to pout.

"Not this time."

"That's brutal dude," Finn said, shaking his head.

"Sorry bro," I smiled, "patting his back. We need you here."

"I like the plan, Riles," Sissie chimed in. "You go after the thieves, and we'll keep our eyes on Charlotte."

"How's that sound to you, grandpa?" I asked.

"Sounds like a good plan."

"Cool," I smiled. "Wish me luck!"

Then, I reached for the book and in a white flash, grandpa's kitchen disappeared.

***

Quickly, the two thieves headed straight to the canyon. They were nearly shaking in fear from the flashes of light and Layla's outburst. The stranger who flashed white had called her by another name. *Was it Lark?* Not that it mattered. This job was getting worse by the minute.

It didn't take long to reach the canyon. They saw Layla's red scarf hung over a rock.

"Alright, we collect the scarf and catch up to Zil at the tomb?" Patrick asked.

Liam nodded.

Patrick slid off his camel, and walked over to the rock. As he tugged at the scarf, it tugged back.

He jumped back, "Did you see that?"

"See what?" Liam asked, looking up from his camel.

"The scarf pulled back."

Liam laughed, "Just get the scarf. This place gives me the creeps."

"I'm not touching it," Patrick grumbled, walking back to the camels.

"Do I have to do everything?" Liam grumbled back.

He slid off his camel and walked toward the scarf, shoving Patrick as he passed.

When Liam grabbed the scarf, it happened again - the scarf tugged back.

Liam jumped back too.

Just then, a flash of white light appeared behind them. The two thieves spun around to see Riles standing just past their camels.

"Hello boys," Riles taunted, hands on his hips.

Liam and Patrick had had enough. Terrified, they glanced at each other, ran for the camels, scrambled into saddles, and raced up the valley floor - away from the scarf, and away from Riles.

Riles chuckled, "That was easy."

Then, sniffing the desert air, Riles thought he smelled coffee.

In a flash of white, he disappeared.

170

## 16

## The First Chamber

I tumbled back into the kitchen sooner than expected.

"That went well," grandpa smiled.

"It sure did," I laughed, "Those guys bailed quick."

"Good idea, tugging the scarf," Sissie added.

"What do you mean?" I asked.

"The way you tugged the scarf back when Liam and Patrick tried to pick it up," little Finn explained. "That was a good idea - it totally freaked them out."

My eyes got a little bigger, and I turned toward grandpa.

"You didn't tug the scarf, did you Riles?" he asked with a strange smile.

"Nope."

"What?" Sissie and Little Finn blurted out at the same time.

"I - I don't know what you're talking about," I said, shaking my head.

Grandpa leaned back and stroked his beard.

"What's going on, grandpa?" little Finn asked.

"I'm not sure yet," he said softly, "but I have a few ideas."

It didn't look like he wanted to share those ideas with us, so we begged him to keep reading.

He slid up his reading glasses, found his place, and continued.

\*\*\*

As Liam and Patrick sped back toward Luxor, Zil and Charlotte searched for the tomb's entrance. The canyon walls had narrowed, and the stone walls on either side began to look carved. It began with a drawing here and there, but soon, the sides of the canyon resembled large bricks, like a corridor leading deeper into the desert.

The ground has also changed, from sand, to smooth stone, like an ancient path laid by skilled craftsman. Charlotte felt they had to be close.

She stopped to think.

"What is it?" Zil asked. "Have we arrived?"

Charlotte remained silent, lost in thought.

"Well?" Zil prodded.

"We must be close," Charlotte spoke in a whisper, "but something's off."

"What?"

Then, she repeated part of the poem:

*The place not hewn, he rests beneath stone.*
*Do you seek his tomb? Is your heart like his own?*

"The stone walls here are hewn - beautifully carved to depict tombs."

"So, this isn't it?"

Ignoring Zil, Charlotte continued to think. *Place not hewn. Rests beneath stone.*

"That's it!" she squealed with excitement.

Scanning the path, she spotted several large stones cluttering the otherwise smooth path.

"Here Dr. Amenti," Charlotte went on, "Help me with these."

"The uncarved rocks?"

"Exactly," Charlotte exclaimed. "The place not hewn!"

Zil hurried over. They scraped dirt away from the edges of the stones, and rocked them back and forth to work them loose. As they rocked the stones, small bits of sand fell between the cracks, into the earth.

"There's an opening beneath the stones," Zil shouted with excitement.

A small shaft of afternoon sunlight reached into the opening they had carved. Charlotte and Zil peered into what looked like a small chamber.

They had found it, the entrance to the tomb.

Quickly, they pulled more stones away, clearing a hole large enough to fit their bags. Charlotte lowered her gear. The floor of the chamber looked to be about ten feet down.

They pulled away another stone or two - just enough space to squeeze in.

"Well done, Charlotte," Dr. Amenti applauded.

Charlotte sat with her feet in the opening, but Zil caught her shoulder before she could slide in.

"How will we get out?" Zil called into the chamber.

Charlotte was so excited to get into the chamber, she forgot to consider how she might get out.

"Good thinking, Zil," she said. Let's grab a rope from the supplies and tie it off on this larger stone.

Charlotte and Zil secured the rope, and lowered it into the opening.

"After you," Zil smiled.

Charlotte grabbed the rope and quickly slid down between the stones, rappelling into the dusty, dim lit chamber.

It took a few moments for her eyes to adjust. The afternoon sun colored the room with a single, stale shaft of golden light. Charlotte scanned the chamber in amazement. Thousands of hieroglyphs decorated the walls from floor to ceiling.

Charlotte tugged out her notebook to compare her drawings with the walls.

As she studied the walls, Layla arrived overhead.

She tugged Zil back from the opening, "Things have become more complicated."

"How so?" he in a hushed whisper.

"Another - a white flash - has been watching."

Zil turned his gaze back to the chamber, "We are so close. Can you handle it?"

"Of course, I can handle it," Layla shot back. "That's why I'm here."

Charlotte interrupted them, calling up, "These images match the stories."

Zil leaned into the opening, trying to take it in.

"Are you coming?" Charlotte asked.

"Yes, of course," Zil called down. "Layla has arrived."

Charlotte's heart quickened. She thought of the clue from Elizabeth.

Zil grabbed a supply bag and lowered himself into the chamber. Layla followed with another bag. Zil walked toward Charlotte while Layla pulled a torch from one of the supply bags and lit it.

"What now?" he asked.

"If my notes are correct," Charlotte spoke softly, while still comparing her notes to the walls, "there will be four doors in this chamber - one along each wall."

Zil grabbed the torch from Layla and started to walk the perimeter of the room.

"What exactly are we looking for?" he asked.

Layla took a second torch and lit it.

178

"Only one of the doors will lead to the next chamber. The others will be traps," Charlotte spoke while reading through her notes. "We have to decide which door is the correct - which door would the Forgotten Pharaoh choose."

Zil came to what looked like a tall doorway decorated with regal drawings. A worn wooden door sealed the opening. To the left and right, drawings depicted hundreds of Egyptians cowering before the door. Their eyes wide, their bodies afraid.

*Imagine that power*, Zil thought with a wicked smile. *They will do whatever he says - they fear him.*

As Zil examined the wall, Charlotte checked her notes and whispered the poem again, to herself:

*The place not hewn, he rests beneath stone.*
*Do you seek his tomb? Is your heart like his own?*

*From poverty to power, with love fighting fear,*
*Seek the cooling air, his body rests near.*

"This is the door for a King," Zil declared, stepping back.

"We don't have time for this, Zil," Layla scolded, pushing him aside. "Is this the door or not?"

"It must be," Zil confirmed, realizing he was one step closer to finding the Forgotten Pharaoh.

Charlotte looked up, still thinking on the second stanza. *He wasn't like other kings. He didn't rule by fear!*

"Wait!" she called out, but it was too late.

# 17

## The Second Test

Layla ran toward the wall and pushed through the door. As she did, a flurry of bats poured into the chamber. Layla disappeared, screaming in a flash of red. Bats overwhelmed the room, swooping this way and that. Zil and Charlotte dropped to the floor, covering their heads with their hands.

The sound was deafening. Screaming bats filled the chamber. Zil and Charlotte's hearts raced as they waited for the flurry to end.

Finally, the bats found their way out, exiting through the space overhead.

Both Zil and Charlotte continued to lie on the floor, frozen in fear. After a few moments of quiet - Charlotte glanced around the room to be sure it was safe.

Rising carefully to her feet, she asked, "Where's Layla?"

"I'm not sure," Zil replied, standing up and dusting his pants. He reached for his torch, lying nearby, still burning.

The two archaeologists walked slowly toward the door Layla had pushed through. Beyond the opening, the room dropped off like a cliff, revealing a gigantic cave. Hot, dry air swept up from the cave and into the doorway. Far below, they could see Layla's torch still burning on a stone floor.

Behind them, a second flash of red light, and Layla reappeared.

"I thought you said that was the correct door!" Layla screamed at Zil.

Charlotte stepped back against the wall, trying to understand.

"I thought it was!" Zil hollered back, with a bit of fear in the back of his voice.

Charlotte watched as the two villains sparred. She had seen a flash like that when Elizabeth appeared. That flash had been white. Did Layla have the same power?

Done with Zil, Layla turned to Charlotte.

"Well, Miss Cook," she chided. "We are running out of time. How did you know that door was wrong?"

***

"Grandpa," Sissie interrupted, "I think Charlotte's getting pretty scared."

"Yeah," Little Finn piped in, "We need to help her. Lark's tough."

The book flashed white. It seemed to agree.

"Listen," I chimed in, "we can't really send her a note, since Lark's with her. And if we jump in now, it'll just make things worse. Charlotte's tough too. Let's keep reading and see what happens."

Finn tilted his head - he must have thought I was crazy.

Sissie looked at me while she took it all in. After a few seconds, she nodded.

"That's probably a good plan. What do you think grandpa?"

"Sounds good to me," he smiled. "We don't have to worry about those thieves, so I think we've got a good chance of saving this story."

"I think so too," I said with a smile.

Sissie and Finn agreed, and grandpa continued to read.

\*\*\*

Charlotte tugged out her notebook, and opened it to a page of doors. There were four images across the page. One looked like the door Layla pushed open. Two looked similar, showing a king with lots of power, surrounded by Egyptians who looked afraid.

In the fourth picture, the door looked much different - shorter, and surrounded by Egyptian families, grouped together. The people looked joyful and friendly.

Charlotte pointed at the picture of the fourth door, and recited the second stanza of the poem again:

*From poverty to power, with love fighting fear,*
*Seek the cooling air, his body rests near.*

"I believe," she continued, "we're looking for a doorway like this."

Zil circled the room looking at the other doorways.

"Here," he motioned for Layla and Charlotte to join.

Holding the torches toward the door, they compared it to the drawing in Charlotte's notebook: shorter, and surrounded by happy images of families.

"Love fighting fear," she whispered.

Layla groaned at Charlotte's comment, and pushed the door with her torch. It didn't budge.

She tried again, nothing. Zil handed his torch to Charlotte and pushed with both arms - all his strength. Still, the door didn't budge.

Handing the torch back to Zil, reviewed her notebook again. *Poverty to power*, she thought.

"Yes, of course."

Charlotte knelt down at the door, and ran her fingers along the base. She could feel cool air pushing strong from the other side.

"It's cold inside - seek the cooling air. I think we need to pull this door, not push it."

Tucking her fingers under the door, Charlotte tugged at the base of the door. With just a little force, she felt it loosen.

"Here we go," she warned, and with a second tug, the door swung open.

Behind it, came a rush of cold air, blowing out both torches.

With the sun beginning to set, light in the chamber had grown even dimmer. Without the torches, Layla, Zil, and Charlotte could barely see into the cool passage. Standing in the doorway, they could still feel the steady cold wind.

Charlotte shivered.

"What next, Miss Cook?" Layla bullied.

Since seeing Riles, Lark had been anxious to find the treasure and finish this miserable mission. *Liam and Patrick should be here by now*, she thought. Every minute they were late, she grew a bit more anxious - a bit more worried.

This mission mattered. Master Calamitous told her how important this story was to him. She couldn't let him down. Not again. Not because of that white flash rookie.

Charlotte closed her notebook - it was too dark to read anyway. She tucked it into her coat pocket and pointed into the passage.

"Next, we walk."

"After you," Zil said with a cruel smile.

Charlotte realized this little game was winding down. Once they found the treasure, Layla and Zil would have no need for her. But, she trusted Elizabeth, so she ducked enough to get in the door, and walked down the passage with a strange sense of hope and strength.

Things were going to be okay.

She could feel it.

# 18

## Dark To Light

Charlotte's eyes watered in the cold wind, so she closed them. Inside the doorway, she stood tall, and stretched out her arms, reaching toward the sides. The narrow passage had smooth cut walls. Charlotte imagined that they were painted as wonderfully as the walls in the outside chamber.

She listened to the footsteps of Layla and Zil following behind her. The passage seemed to descend gradually, taking them deeper into the canyon.

As they walked, the passage also narrowed. The air became cooler, and it seemed to move faster. It also became louder. She lost track of Layla and Zil, focusing on the path ahead.

Rather than blowing directly at them, the air now seemed to be blowing from higher up.

Charlotte's right hand came to the end of the right wall. She paused. The flow of cool air felt strong, blowing down at them. Keeping her left hand against the left wall, and holding her right hand in front of her body, Charlotte took a few more steps.

Suddenly, her hand pushed past the breeze. She pulled her hand back to her body - the breeze still flowed. Reaching ahead, her hand pushed past the air again. Eyes shut tight, she smiled. They were getting closer.

Charlotte took a few more steps. She passed the cold air. She could still hear it behind her. A few more steps, and her right hand felt a wall ahead of her.

She opened her eyes. No difference. The passage remained absolutely black.

Charlotte followed the corner with her left hand, took a few more steps forward, and extended her right hand toward the right - she felt another wall, a turn. She could hear Zil and Layla stepping past the airflow behind her.

"Miss Cook? Miss Cook?" Zil barked, with a small tremor in his voice.

"Stop shouting," Layla shouted back, "She can't be far ahead!"

"I'm just glad to be done with that wind," Zil barked back. "Miss Cook?"

"I'm over here," Charlotte answered into the darkness. "The passage turns just after the wind stops."

"This is impossible," Layla complained. "We'll never get a torch past that wind, and we can't see a thing without light."

Charlotte smiled, though nobody could see it in the blackness. Layla's complaint reminded her of the last stanza in the poem:

*Your longing for adventure has almost found a cure,*
*Where dark retreats from light, you'll find him buried here.*

"What would make darkness retreat from light?" Charlotte whispered to herself.

"What's that?" Zil asked over the now faint hum of air flowing into the upper passage.

"Of course," Charlotte continued to whisper in hushed excitement, "it's the next clue."

"What clue?" Layla asked.

Charlotte didn't reply. Instead, she began feeling every inch of the wall as systematically as possible. She started where her left hand had felt the corner.

*It'll be right after the air*, she thought.

"What's the next clue?" Zil asked over the faint hum of air.

"Where dark retreats from light," she replied quickly.

"What does that mean?" he asked.

Charlotte smiled again. Her left hand had found part of the answer. A smooth loose rock in the wall. She removed the rock and reached her arm into the opening. All the way at the back, with her elbow nearly inside the wall, she felt the end of a rope.

She pulled it.

In the same moment, the wall to her left lowered, and the air flow stopped.

"What happened?" Layla barked.

Charlotte waited.

Where the wall had been, she heard a different sound - like rope rubbing back and forth along wood. Then, the darkness gave way to a spark, then another. Each small spark briefly lighting the tight passage corner - briefly revealing the large bowstring contraption hidden in the wall.

Then, the spark caught fire.

Within the wall, one spark turned to flame, and the flame raced up several dusty lines to the left and right. Those lines met new lines close to the ceiling, running both directions along the passage - both where they had been, and where they were going.

Charlotte reveled in the beauty of the spark against utter darkness.

Then, before the tiny fire burned out, it found a torch hung overhead, still alive with oil. Passing first torches, the lines ran on to the next torch - as if veins of electricity connected the tunnels of ancient Egypt.

All the while, the light grew brighter. All the while, the darkness retreated.

"The last clue," Charlotte exclaimed, giddy with delight.

*\*\**

"She did it!" Sissie enthusiastically interrupted.

"Indeed, she did," Grandpa smiled.

"She's not out of the woods yet guys!" I said.

"You mean out of the tomb?" Finn asked.

We all laughed.

"Seriously, guys," I chuckled. "Can we see what happens next? She still might need our help."

"Of course," grandpa replied, and he continued reading.

*\*\**

With the tunnel lit, Zil, Layla, and Charlotte made their way through several more turns, to the end of the passage. Torches lit the whole corridor.

At the end of the passage, they came to a large stone door. The walls to the left and right had no drawings on them, and a single carving decorated the center of the stone entrance. The carving looked like a human chest and neck - the Egyptian symbol for the heart.

They all paused in front of the door. Charlotte had worked so hard - studying and waiting years - for this very moment. This had to be the lost tomb of the Forgotten Pharaoh.

Zil too had been waiting, happy to use Charlotte for his own victory. In a moment, it would all be his.

Charlotte paused to review the poem her father had taught her:

*The place not hewn, he rests beneath stone.*
*Do you seek his tomb? Is your heart like his own?*

*From poverty to power, with love fighting fear,*

*Seek the cooling air, his body rests near.*

*Friend beware, only seek the tomb for right,*
*Forget not his heart, or you will face his might.*

*Your longing for adventure has almost found a*
*cure,*
*Where dark retreats from light, you'll find him*
*buried here.*

Layla moved quickly toward the door - anxious to complete her mission, worried about interruptions, and ready to finally please her Master.

"Wait!" Charlotte exclaimed.

Layla froze. She didn't want to fall into a cave full of bats a second time.

"What?" she barked at Charlotte.

"Why a heart?" Charlotte asked.

Layla glanced at the door and then back toward Charlotte.

"Why is the only image on the door a heart?" Charlotte repeated.

"Wasn't there something about a heart in the poem?" Zil asked.

"Yes," Charlotte replied.

She recited the poem again. Her words hung in the air.

"Is your heart like his own?" she emphasized. "Forget not his heart, or you will face his might."

"What does it all mean?" Zil asked.

Charlotte thought she knew what the heart meant.

She remembered the stories her father told - of a good king. He came from humble roots and rose to power in all the right ways. He served his people with kindness and compassion. He shared his power - and wealth - rather than hoarding it for himself.

In short, he was good. Zil and Layla, on the other hand, were not.

"Who cares?" Layla grumbled. "Let's finish this."

She grabbed a torch from the wall and with a push, Layla shoved the stone door wide open. Hints of glittering treasure danced in the torchlight. The corners of the room remained hidden in darkness.

They had finally reached the tomb and it smelled a bit like coffee.

## 19

## Heart and Might

"Coffee?" Sissie interrupted with a squeal.

"No way!" Finn blurted out.

"How'd the tall man get inside the tomb?" I asked, expecting grandpa to have an answer.

Grandpa lowered the book wearing a quizzical expression.

"It doesn't matter how he got there," Sissie interrupted again. "If he's there, we need to help Charlotte. I promised her I'd have her back. I need to get in the story, and now!"

The book flashed a bit brighter, and Sissie looked to grandpa for approval.

"Are you certain you want in?" grandpa asked.

"Yes," Sissie answered quickly, her breath and heartrate quickening with excitement.

"What about Lark?" I asked.

"I can handle her," Sissie replied. "Just let me at her."

With that, she reached out for the book and disappeared in a flash of bright white light.

"Grandpa?" Little Finn and I urged.

He seemed lost in thought.

"Oh, yes, sorry," he nodded, found his place, and continued to read.

***

They had finally reached the tomb and it smelled a bit like coffee.

Suddenly, white light flashed in the tomb, blinding the three explorers, and the tomb door slammed shut.

The instant Sissie had appeared – in the center of the tomb – she saw a silhouette slam the door shut. Then, strong hands grabbed her and shoved her through a side door, into a smaller, even darker room. A hand pressed against her mouth, keeping her from screaming. The hand smelled like coffee.

Then, the hands spun her around. Her back pressed against the wall. She faced a mysterious man wearing a scarf and a thick turban. His left hand covered Sissie's mouth, and as her eyes adjusted to the darkness, she realized his right index finger hovered in front of his scarf.

He wanted her to remain quiet.

Her heart raced. He smelled like coffee.

She wanted to scream.

She raised her eyebrows and nodded a little, letting him know she would stay quiet.

Slowly and carefully, he unwrapped his scarf and lowered it. Sissie's gasped. Her heart continued to race, but she tried to stay completely still.

Outside, she could hear the explorers.

Layla was the first to recover, half expecting something like this to happen.

"Zil, help me with this door," she shouted, jumping to her feet. She ran into the room and swung the torch around to light up the corners. No one.

*Riles has to be here somewhere*, Layla thought.

Zil grabbed a torch of his own and stepped into the room behind Layla, cautiously examining the tomb. He certainly didn't want to run into anybody who flashed unless it was absolutely necessary.

Inside, the tomb of the Forgotten Pharaoh looked similar to the first chamber – a doorway on each wall. Two of the doors were open. The one they entered through, and the door to their left.

*He must be in there*, Layla thought, eyeing the other open door.

She ran straight to the open door and slammed it shut. A wicked smile crawled onto her face.

*That'll hold him.*

Layla felt certain she had trapped Riles behind the door. But the white flash hadn't been Riles.

It had been Sissie.

Inside, the man slowly lowered his hand from Sissie's face.

"Father," Sissie whispered. "What are *you* doing here?"

***

"Hold on, grandpa," I interrupted. "Did you just read what I think you read?"

"Yes."

"Wait, so daddy's the coffee guy?" little Finn chimed in.

"It looks that way," grandpa sighed. "May I continue?"

We nodded. Grandpa found his place and kept reading.

***

"Father," Sissie whispered. "What are you doing here?"

"I should ask you the same thing," he whispered back. "But we don't have time for that right now. Stay safe, protect Charlotte, and I'll see you soon."

If there had been enough light, she would have seen him wink. Then, he disappeared in a bright flash of white light.

With fresh confidence, Sissie ran to the door and shoved it open, nearly knocking Lark to the ground.

In a flash of red, she had regained her feet and locked arms with Elizabeth.

"You must be the sister I've heard so much about."

Elizabeth didn't answer, she just held her ground.

"You think you can save Charlotte? Save this story?"

Lark pressed forward, pinning Sissie against the wall. Holding her there, Lark stared at her. Sissie tried to press back, but Lark was too strong. Sissie looked away. Lark laughed, and shoved Sissie to the ground. Sissie slumped, defeated.

Zil closed in, holding a torch.

"She's another one?" he asked.

"Yes," Lark laughed again. "But, not much to worry about."

Charlotte ran over to comfort Elizabeth. Zil laughed.

"Are you okay?" Charlotte asked.

Sissie sighed, "Yes, I'm fine, but I wanted to help you get the treasure. I don't think I'm strong enough."

"Don't worry about the treasure," Charlotte whispered. "It shouldn't leave this room anyway."

"But I thought you wanted it?" Sissie whispered back.

"I thought so too, but now I'm not so sure," Charlotte paused. "I think it's enough to see it - to know the stories were real.

While they talked, Zil and Layla continued to survey the room. Then, Zil ran out of the passage, returning a few minutes later with empty supply bags from the first chamber.

"You fill these bags," Layla ordered, "and we'll come back for the rest when Liam and Patrick catch up. Understand?"

"Yes, of course," Zil agreed.

"You can start with this," Layla said, picking up a simple crown of gold and tossing it to Dr. Amenti.

As soon as Layla touched the crown, all four of them heard a loud crack and the room began to shake.

"What'd you do?" Zil barked at her, with a hint of panic in his voice.

"You saw what I did," Layla hollered back. "I tossed you a crown."

Charlotte helped Sissie to her feet. It was time to go. She knew exactly what was happening.

"It's your heart," Charlotte shouted back toward Layla. "Remember the poem:

*Friend beware, only seek the tomb for right,*
*Forget not his heart, or you will face his might.*

As she spoke, the shake turned to quake, and the room began to fill with dust and falling stone.

Angry at the thought of failing, Layla yelled at Zil to hurry, and turned her attention back to Elizabeth and Charlotte. This was her chance to finish things for good. She wasn't about to let Elizabeth spoil things for her.

Just then, a flash of white blinded them. Layla found herself face to face with the tall man who smells like coffee. With one hand, he grabbed ahold of Layla. With the other, he pointed to the door.

"Go," he said over his shoulder. "Now!"

## 20

## Home Again

Sissie didn't skip a beat. She grabbed Charlotte by the arm and in a flash, they disappeared. In a second flash, they were standing in the first chamber. Charlotte giggled with the excitement of flashing from one spot to another. In a second flash, they were standing overhead in the narrow canyon.

Charlotte laughed out loud.

"That was amazing!"

Sissie smiled back, proud.

The two girls hurried up the canyon toward the remaining camel.

Still in the cave below, Lark faced off with the tall man.

"Another white flash?" she mocked, trying to shake her arm free.

"Careful, little one, this doesn't have to be your battle," he replied, letting her arm go free.

"You have no idea who I work for," Lark shot back.

"Calamitous?" the tall man asked, through dust and falling rock.

"Master Calamitous," Lark shouted back, "and I can't disappoint him again."

With that, she grabbed hold of Zil, and disappeared in a flash of red light.

The tall man looked around the shaking treasure room with a knowing smile.

"You are not forgotten," he whispered, and in a flash of white, he was gone.

***

"This is crazy!" I exclaimed.

I could hardly contain myself. Dad was in the story with Sissie? I didn't know he even knew about Story Keeping! All of a sudden, I find out he's awesome at it? What a morning!

Little Finn couldn't believe it either.

"Boys," grandpa interrupted our side conversation, "the story's not over just yet. Shall we finish, so Sissie can get home?

"Definitely," Finn agreed. "Then, you and father have some serious explaining to do."

"Mom's not in on this too, is she?" I asked.

Grandpa ignored my question, hid his face in the book, and continued reading.

***

In a red flash, Lark and Dr. Amenti reappeared at the first chamber. The ground continued to shake, and much of the ceiling had crumbled, leaving a staircase of boulders rising to the canyon floor.

Zil's heart raced, and his knees shook. As much as he wanted the treasure, he had no interest in heading back down the dark, cold passage while the ceiling continued to collapse.

Luckily, he had held tight to one supply bag when Lark flashed him out of the room. He glanced into the bag - it still held the crown.

Layla and Zil scrambled up the rubble to the main canyon. From their they headed toward the camels. When they arrived, they found one camel, with Charlotte and Elizabeth atop the mount.

"Just where do you think you're going?" Layla demanded.

"Home," Charlotte answered.

In a flash of white, Elizabeth landed in front of Layla. Behind them, the entire canyon shook, and crumbling stone buried the path to the tomb.

"You see, Lark, it's over," Sissie said. "The treasure is buried, and Charlotte has escaped."

"Not all the treasure," Dr. Amenti taunted, raising the crown out of the bag.

Sissie saw the opportunity and seized it. In a series of flashes, she grabbed the crown, handed it to Charlotte, and reappeared in front of Lark.

Then Sissie locked arms with Lark, as Charlotte sped away on the camel.

"Now, it's really over," she said. "Go home."

Lark snarled, but Sissie was right. It *was* over. Her stomach turned at the thought of facing Master Calamitous empty handed. In a flash of red, she disappeared. Sissie flashed too, and reappeared on the camel with Charlotte, galloping toward Luxor.

Dr. Amenti, unable to flash from one place to another, spent the whole, long night walking back to Luxor empty handed.

Charlotte and Elizabeth, on the other hand, had a wonderful return journey.

They made their way by camel to Luxor. There, they boarded a steamship to Cairo. When they arrived in Cairo, they visited the Egyptian National Museum. She told her story to the authorities, and Dr. Amenti was fired straight away. Charlotte donated the crown to the museum, believing it should remain in Egypt. Sissie approved.

From there, the two friends boarded a train to Alexandria, where Sissie watched as Charlotte re-board the RMS Homeric - that tired trans-Atlantic cruise ship that would take her back to England.

Sissie enjoyed her time with Charlotte - it had been fun to make a true friend, and she was sad to see Charlotte's boat leave the harbor.

Taking one last look around the port of Alexandria, Sissie smiled. It had been quite an adventure. Then, in a flash of bright white, she was gone.

\*\*\*

In a bundle of white light, Sissie tumbled back into the kitchen, exhausted.

I threw my arms around her for a quick hug.

"Good to have you back, sis!" I said.

"Way to go, Sissie!" little Finn chimed in.

Grandpa set the book down, closed it, and nodded approvingly.

"Well done, Elizabeth," he said softly. "I imagine you have some questions for me?"

"You bet we do!" we all shot back.

"Did you know that father was in the story?"

"I had my suspicions," grandpa replied.

"Was he the flash of light I saw in Charlotte's hotel room?"

"I believe so," grandpa nodded. "Yes."

"Did he tug on the scarf?" little Finn asked.

"I believe so," grandpa nodded. "Yes again."

"I still can't believe he was the tall man who smelled like coffee this whole time," I shook my head. "How come they never told us about story keeping? And, why was he in the same story as us?"

"Excellent questions, Riles," grandpa said with a sigh. "Unfortunately, I think it means something has gone wrong."

My head tilted slightly. *Something wrong?* I wondered. Grandpa looked distant, concentrated.

Just then, a loud "thud" shook the house.

It sounded like the "thump" we heard earlier in the morning. We froze.

"What was that, grandpa? Little Finn whispered.

Grandpa put his finger over his lips. We listened.

"Was it something in the basement?" I asked.

"Is it father?" Sissie asked.

"Perhaps," grandpa spoke quietly. "And, if it is he may have answers. Follow me."

Grandpa had a curious look on his face – serious and maybe a bit concerned.

He stood up from the table and grabbed a frying pan in the kitchen. Holding it like a sword, he headed down the hall, toward the basement steps. We followed close behind.

Sissie grabbed my arm and squeezed it tight. Little Finn tucked in behind grandpa's leg.

Grandpa paused at the basement door. He dug a bulky keychain out of his pocket, and sliding the keys between his fingers, selected one. Grandpa always kept the basement door locked. None of us had ever been down there before. He fit the key into the lock and turned it.

The door stuck a bit and then creaked open.

Cold air snuck up the staircase from the basement raising goosebumps up and down my arms. It smelled musty like old books and camping gear. We heard the soft sound of quiet whispers below.

We tiptoed, following grandpa through the doorway and slowly down steep wooden steps. At every creak, grandpa paused, and then continued.

Suddenly, the whispers stopped.

We froze.

Then, a flash of bright white lit the room below.

Grandpa hustled down the last few steps and turned into the basement. We followed close, not wanting to be left behind.

Grandpa moved quickly toward a square, wooden table in the center of the room. Two open books glowed on the table top, and two mugs rested to the side, still steaming. Two chairs had been pushed back from the table.

Grandpa stood over the table, taking it all in. He chuckled softly and let out a sigh.

"What in the world do they think they're doing?" he said to himself, but loud enough for us to hear.

"They?" I whispered.

"Your parents."

Grandpa flipped the first book closed. We recognized the sandy brown binding and thick border of hieroglyphs at once.

They had been reading Charlotte's story.

# Bonus Chapter

## From Deep Sea Pirates

Afternoon light filtered into grandpa's basement. Grandpa sat at the square wooden table, rubbing his chin. On the table, two mugs still steamed with fresh tea. One book, Charlotte's, rested closed in front of grandpa. Across the table, another book sat open, bubbling with bright light.

I looked around the room. Grandpa's basement felt like a military bunker from the Cold War – dark, dusty, probably safe, and full of important stuff. He probably had survival supplies hidden somewhere.

Massive bookcases lined two of the walls. The shelves overflowed with books and file boxes –

all different shapes, sizes, and colors. Behind grandpa, a rolling chalkboard rested in front of another wall. Unfamiliar mathematical equations and strange symbols filled it from edge to edge. The final wall held all kinds of photos, maps, and newspaper clippings. Giant, old rugs covered most of the cement floor.

The three of us watched grandpa for a few moments. Then we started exploring.

Finn headed straight to the bookcases – hoping to find more glowing books.

Sissie drifted toward the chalkboard.

I was drawn to a desk below the newspaper clippings.

Piles of handwritten notes mixed with pages from old books covered the top of the desk. Some of the notes looked like grandpa's writing. Some looked like mom and dad's writing. Some I didn't recognize.

The open books looked special – and really old. They didn't have any pictures in them. None of them seemed to glow, but I didn't want to touch them just in case. What did it all mean?

I glanced over my shoulder at grandpa, still sitting in his chair thinking.

Underneath the desk I found several cardboard boxes stuffed with electronics – circuits and fuses wired this way and that, radios and phones pulled apart and strung back together with loose wiring.

My imagination bubbled – was grandpa building something? Was father or mother?

I looked over at grandpa again. This time, he looked up from his thinking and winked at me.

*He's letting us explore*, I thought. *What does he want us to find? Another adventure?*

Sissie stepped back from the chalkboard and joined me at the desk. She scanned the messy collection of maps, photos, and news clippings smattered on the wall. Little bits of string hung between the scraps, connecting them. They hung like flies in a spider web, clues for a detective.

Something tied them together – somehow this wall told a story.

We examined the wall clippings together in silence. After a few moments, grandpa joined us, standing quietly behind us. Little Finn still seemed content to search the bookcases.

"Look," I whispered under my breath, raising my hand toward the top left of the wall.

I pointed to a photo of what looked like shelves in an old book store.

I recognized the leather-bound adventure propped up on the shelf. It was Drift's story. I could see the planets on its cover.

My finger followed a piece of red string stretching from that photo to a newspaper clipping. It appeared to be some kind of advertisement:

"Seekers and Keepers another calling is found. Leather bound, $500."

"Five-hundred dollars?" Sissie whispered. "That's an expensive book."

"It's a special one, as you know," grandpa whispered from behind us.

My finger traced another string - one connecting the advertisement to a city map. The map showed a city with a river winding through the center. Lots of strings stretched like sun rays from that city map.

"That must be an important city," I whispered.

"Uh-huh," She whispered back.

Grandpa sighed, lost in memories of his own.

"Is that mom and dad?" Sissie asked, pointing toward the middle of the wall.

"I think so, but that must have been taken a long time ago," I whispered back.

"Yes," grandpa said quietly, "just after your parents met, at university."

I wondered to myself, *Did mom and dad know about Story Keeping way back then?*

My eyes drifted from that picture to so many others – strings linking people and articles, books, and maps.

One, a picture of a girl and an older man walking in a park, caught my attention. The people were small and a bit blurry, walking near the back of the photo. The man wore a long dark coat and a hat that shadowed his face. The girl looked familiar. Could it be?

"Lark?" The name slipped out under my breath. Only Sissie heard it.

She looked at me and then scanned the wall.

"You're right, it is her," she whispered back.

I nodded, my eyes still holding on to the photo.

"Grandpa, who are these people? What is all this?" the words snuck out of my throat in another whisper.

He looked toward the picture of the man and the girl.

"Do you recognize them?" he replied quietly.

"Yes, well, some of them."

I did. I just couldn't believe it.

What was a picture of Lark doing in my grandpa's basement? And, who was the man walking with her in the park?

"The girl looks like Lark," Sissie whispered.

Grandpa nodded, "That's correct."

"Did you take that photo?" I asked.

"No."

"Did you put all this stuff on the wall?" I asked.

"Some of it," grandpa replied cautiously.

As we whispered, little Finn joined us.

"What is all this?" he asked in his best attempt at a whisper.

"Children," grandpa started in, "you are only starting to learn about story keeping."

"But you've been teaching us all week?" Sissie interrupted.

"My dear Elizabeth," grandpa answered, "It has only been a few days since our first story.

You are only starting to understand - to meet our friends and foes in these strange adventures."

"I'm not meeting anyone," Finn blurted out, "because you won't let me in any stories."

Grandpa placed his hand on Finn's shoulder, "You are still young, little one. You don't need to be in such a hurry to grow up."

"I just want to go on an adventure like everyone else," he pouted, folding his arms and headed back to the bookcase.

Grandpa turned back to Sissie and I.

"It looks like your father and mother have moved into another story. I didn't expect them to visit Charlotte's story, but I'm sure they have their reasons."

"So, they jumped into the other book?" I asked.

"I believe so."

Though we didn't know it at the time, little Finn heard grandpa's whispers.

"Can we read it?" Sissie asked.

Though we didn't see it at the time, little Finn had drifted toward the square, wooden table to examine the open book.

"I'm not sure that's a good idea," grandpa said, lowering his voice. "It's not a very safe book."

"Did you say father and mother jumped into this book?" Little Finn asked from behind us.

Grandpa, Sissie and I spun around. Little Finn was on a chair, leaning across the table, hovering over the open book as it bubbled bright with light.

"What are you doing?" I hollered.

"I'm tired of not having my own adventure," little Finn said with a mischievous smile.

"Finn don't!" grandpa said, lunging for the table, but it was too late.

In a flash of white, little Finn was gone.

# Ready for more Story Keeping?

I know what you're thinking: "It can't end there!"

Don't worry, it doesn't.

Find out what happens next...

- ✓ Will our Story Keeping heroes jump into another book?
- ✓ Will they meet Agent Lark again?
- ✓ What about Master Calamitous? Is he still trying to ruin happy endings?
- ✓ Does Grandpa know more than he is telling?
- ✓ And where did their parents really go that summer?

## Two Requests:

1. Would you be willing to leave a review on Amazon? It'd be a HUGE help!

2. Don't forget to snag your FREE GIFT at *www.armarshall.com/storykeeping*

18026778R00142

Made in the USA
San Bernardino, CA
20 December 2018